What Teens A[re Saying about]
DIARY OF A TEENAGE GIRL

"I don't know how you write these books, because it's like you're looking into the life of every teenage Christian girl.... Thank you so much for these books. I feel like God has truly blessed me with them."

"I'd just like to thank you for writing something that is so close to real life. I pray that it'll really get to someone's heart like it did to mine."

"I've read the Caitlin books, and they have helped me SO much.... Her life challenges me to be more like God. Thank you for writing these books so that teens like me can be encouraged."

"I'm not much of a reader, but Melody Carlson is an amazing author who caught my interest, and I never want the series to end."

"Diary of A Teenage Girl books are the best ever!! Between my best friend and me, we have all nine books and can't wait for the first Kim book to be released!"

"Since reading these books, I have become bolder in my faith and with reaching out to those around me. Thank you for accepting God's call on your life—He is blessing you!"

"These are the greatest books of all time! They've really gotten me thinking about my relationship with God. Melody Carlson totally understands us girls, and I fully respect that!"

Diary of a Teenage Girl

Kim Book N°. 3

Falling Up

a novel

MELODY CARLSON

Multnomah Books

FALLING UP
published by Multnomah Books
and in association with the literary agency of Sara A. Fortenberry

© 2006 by Carlson Management Co., Inc.
International Standard Book Number: 978-1-59052-324-7

Cover design by Studiogearbox.com
Cover photo by PixelWorks Studios, www.ShootPW.com

Published in the United States by WaterBrook Multnomah, an imprint of the
Crown Publishing Group, a division of Random House Inc., New York.

MULTNOMAH and its mountain colophon are registered trademarks
of Random House Inc.

Printed in the United States of America

For information:
MULTNOMAH BOOKS
12265 ORACLE BOULEVARD, SUITE 200
COLORADO SPRINGS, CO 80921

Library of Congress Cataloging-in-Publication Data
Carlson, Melody.
Falling up : a novel / Melody Carlson.
    p. cm. -- (Diary of a teenage girl. Kim)
ISBN 1-59052-324-5
   Summary: Dealing with her grief over her mother's recent death and major
problems her family and friends are facing cause Kim so much stress she even finds
it hard to pray, but things improve when she really starts to "let go and let God."
[1. Grief--Fiction. 2. Christian life--Fiction. 3. Pregnancy--Fiction. 4. Korean
Americans--Fiction. 5. Diaries--Fiction.] I. Title.
   II. Series: Carlson, Melody. Diary of a teenage girl. Kim. PZ7.C216637Fal 2006
   [Fic]--dc22

                             2005025584

11 12 13—10 9 8 7 6 5 4

Books by Melody Carlson:

Piercing Proverbs

DIARY OF A TEENAGE GIRL SERIES
<u>Caitlin O'Conner</u>:
Becoming Me
It's My Life
Who I Am
On My Own
I Do!
<u>Chloe Miller</u>:
My Name Is Chloe
Sold Out
Road Trip
Face the Music
<u>Kim Peterson</u>:
Just Ask
Meant to Be
Falling Up
That Was Then… (June 2006)

TRUECOLORS SERIES
Dark Blue, color me lonely
Deep Green, color me jealous
Torch Red, color me torn
Pitch Black, color me lost
Burnt Orange, color me wasted
Fool's Gold, color me consumed
Blade Silver, color me scarred
Bitter Rose, color me broken

One

Saturday, May 4

I woke up crying last night. Sobbing so hard that my chest hurt. I thought it was a nightmare, although I couldn't recall anything specific, only this heaviness pressing down on me like a bag of rocks, like my world had come to a horrible end.

I tried to shake it off, the way I used to do as a child after a frightening dream. Or else I'd sneak off to my parents' room, crawling into bed with them, always on my mom's side, snuggling up to her and sometimes even warming my cold feet on her. She never once complained.

And then I remembered...<u>Mom is gone</u>. Like a slap in the face I remembered that she had died on Saturday night, prom night, and that her funeral service had been just yesterday. Full realization hit me...<u>my mom is gone,</u>

<u>and she isn't coming back</u>. That's when I started crying all over again. Only harder now.

How long would it take for this to really sink in? And how long until that dull ache deep down inside of me goes away? I got out of bed and started to leave my room, but then I remembered that Maya and Aunt Shannon are still here and that Maya was sleeping in the family room, and I might wake her up if I went tiptoeing around. And after hearing the way she so easily rips into her mom, well, I wasn't eager to disturb this girl or to set myself up for an unnecessary imbroglio (my word for the day; it means a big mess).

So I sat at my computer and caught up my diary. Or so I thought. Mostly I've been sitting here, staring at the blank screen and wishing that this ache would go away. I <u>so</u> miss my mom.

"At least you had a good mom," Maya told me yesterday afternoon, after I'd accidentally stumbled upon her sitting in a chaise lounge on the back deck. I went out there to get away from Shannon, who sat like a hypnotized stone in front of the blaring TV, watching some ridiculous soap opera. Maya explained earlier that Shannon's addicted to that show since she actually had a small role on it back in the early eighties.

"Huh?" I said to Maya as I tried to figure out a graceful exit from the backyard. I considered pretending that I came out here to get something, but what?

"Or so it seems," she added with a dramatic roll of her dark brown eyes. Maya is astonishingly beautiful, the kind of girl people actually stop and stare at. I first noticed that after Mom's funeral. At first I thought it was because she was a stranger, but then I realized it was simply her looks. In a way she reminds me of Halle Berry. Only where Halle's expression is sweet and pretty, Maya's is intense and almost hard looking, even a little frightening if she's really mad about something, which is usually the case.

Realizing that there was no polite way to escape my cranky cousin and remembering my resolution to honor my mother by being kind to her relatives, I decided to just bite the bullet. So preparing myself for whatever, I sat down in the lounge chair next to Maya. At least it was quieter out here. I leaned back and sighed. But I still didn't respond to her comment about our moms. I knew better than to engage by now.

"It's true," she continued, as if looking for an argument, which wasn't surprising. "I can hardly believe that your mom and my mom were actually sisters. It's like your mom was some sort of saint, and my mom—" she laughed now, an evil sort of laugh—"is the devil."

"Your mom's not the devil," I said, instantly regretting involving myself in what would surely prove a futile conversation.

"Like you'd even know."

"Maybe not." But now I felt slightly defensive for Shannon. "Still, I'm guessing that this whole thing is pretty upsetting to her. I mean, making the trip out here after all these years, and then she finds out she's too late to see her only sister. Well, she's got to be feeling pretty bummed, don't you think?"

Maya turned around and stared at me, her expression that of an experienced grown-up looking down on a sadly misinformed child. "See, that's just how much you don't get it, Kim. You have absolutely no idea what you're talking about. This is the story of Shannon's life—a day late and a dollar short. It's just the way that woman operates. Ask anyone who knows her, and they'll agree. My mom's got the lousiest timing imaginable. And that's not even her worst problem. Don't get me going."

Well, I had no idea how to respond to that. So I changed the subject. "You know..." I said, suddenly remembering something. "My mom told me that Shannon had been married to someone famous, but with all that's been going on, I totally forgot to ask who it was."

"Don't bother."

"Why?" I persisted, honestly curious as to whether this was even true or not. By now I knew enough about Shannon to realize that her connection to reality is a bit shaky at best.

"Because it's inconsequential."

"Inconsequential to whom?"

"To you or me or anyone."

I considered this. "So, is this inconsequential person your dad?"

She rolled her eyes again, then picked up an old

magazine on the table between us. She pretended to be
interested as she flipped through its slightly curled pages,
but I seriously doubted that my mom's old "Good
Housekeeping" magazine was that engaging to someone
like her.

Then she abruptly dropped the magazine back
down. "Yes, if you really must know, this inconsequential
person is my dad." She stared at me with those
incredible eyes, her perfectly arched brows pulled
together in a fierce frown. "Satisfied now?"

"Not completely. I'm still curious as to whether or not
he's famous. Like is he someone I would know?"

She just pressed her lips together, shaking her head
as an exasperated sigh escaped. So dramatic.
Sometimes I find it hard to believe this girl is only fifteen.
Then she let loose with some bad language that,
although I'm not fond of it, was starting to sound
familiar, especially coming from her. "Oh, if you must
know…"

I waited.

"Have you ever heard of Nick Stark?"

"You mean the singer Nick Stark?"

"Yeah, the old Nick Stark has-been performer from
the swinging seventies, I've-seen-better-days pop singer."

"I know who that is. But he's not exactly a has-been,
Maya." I felt slightly embarrassed to hear the excitement
in my voice growing, like I was some kind of Nick Stark
groupie, which I am not. "I thought Nick Stark was
making a comeback. I mean, he did the soundtrack for

that hit movie last year—what was it called? The one
with Denzel Washington and what's her name?"

"Yeah, yeah," Maya said with a bored expression.
"His supposedly big comeback. One movie. Big deal."

"But aren't you proud of him?"

She just shrugged.

Then it occurred to me that since Shannon and Nick
were divorced, perhaps Maya wasn't too involved in her
dad's life. "Do you see much of him?"

She laughed, but with no sincere humor. "Yeah,
right."

"So he's not around much?" I tried to inject some
sympathy into my voice.

"Not if Shannon has anything to say about it. Other
than sending his monthly check, Nick keeps a pretty low
profile in our neighborhood. She makes sure of that."

"They don't get along?"

"Like oil and water, cats and dogs, whatever cliché
you can think of. No, they do not get along, Kim. They
are a restraining order or prison sentence waiting to
happen. My mom actually keeps a gun under her
pillow."

"Is she really afraid of him?"

"Afraid?" Maya looked as if she was going to laugh
again. "No, she's not afraid. She keeps the gun just
hoping that he'll show up some night, and she can
pretend like he's a prowler and blow his head off. That's
how much she hates him."

"Oh."

"Yes, that must seem very strange and foreign to someone as protected as you." Maya looked thoroughly disgusted now. "You live out here in middle America with your happy little family in your happy little neighborhood just like some freaking family sitcom." She stood up. "So totally unreal!" Then she stormed away.

And I know it was stupid for me to even react. I mean, why should I care about what someone like Maya thinks? Talk about needing a reality check! But her words just got to me. "Happy little family?" We just lost Mom, for Pete's sake!

But instead of saying anything, I just sat out there and stewed. I really wish that Maya and Shannon would go home. I'm tempted to take money out of my own savings to help them change their tickets so they can be out of our hair and our home for good. But then I had to consider…what would Mom do? What would she want?

So after I cooled off, I reconsidered the news that Nick Stark is like my uncle, or sort of, and found it kind of interesting. But it's not like I can talk about it with Shannon who, according to Maya, hates his guts. And I'm not sure I want to get Maya going on it again, since she pretty much leaps off the deep end without much encouragement. So instead, I did a little investigating of Nick Stark online. And it turned out I was right, he is making a serious comeback in his singing career.

But here's what makes me sort of sad… Mom would've gotten such a big kick out of this news. It's just the kind of thing she would've called up a good friend and enjoyed a good chat over. I wouldn't even be surprised if my parents have some old Nick Stark vinyl records stashed away someplace. I can just imagine Mom dragging them out and making us all listen to them. But then she's not here to have fun with it. She never even had the chance to find out about her famous "relative."

On second thought, she might not have liked all the family feuding that came with getting to know our "extended" family. And she'd probably feel sad to learn that Shannon is so bitter about her ex and that she and Maya are always at such odds.

Still, I think she would've gotten a kick out of a famous brother-in-law. Even if he is an ex. But maybe she's well aware of all this by now. I mean, wouldn't God let her in on all these sorts of interesting developments up in heaven? Or maybe no one cares about stuff like that up there. Who knows? It's too much for my little brain to think about. Especially at 3:14 AM.

But before I make another attempt to go to sleep, I think I'll write a letter about my relatives to Jamie—the answer girl. See what she has to say.

Dear Jamie,

My mom recently died, and her sister and niece are staying with my family for several more days. The problem, besides the fact that I desperately miss my mom, is that these two relatives are making me totally crazy with their constant bickering and fighting and general nastiness. To the point that I'd use my own money to change their return tickets, just to get rid of them. Would this be rude?

Unhappy Host

Dear Unhappy,

I'm sorry for your loss. That must be really hard. And having cantankerous relatives can't make it any easier. But instead of wasting your own money, why don't you make sure you give yourself time and space away from these rude relatives? It's not like you have to take care of them 24–7, right? And don't feel responsible for them or their personal problems. I'm sure that's not what your mother would want you to do. Remember, you can't fix everyone.

Just Jamie

Wow, I'm thinking after I finish that, <u>Jamie is right</u>. Okay, I realize that I am Jamie—well, sort of. Sometimes it feels like she's a totally different person, and I get worried that I could possibly develop a personality disorder as a result of taking her too seriously, which I'm determined not to do. However, I do think I'll try to keep her advice in mind for the rest of Shannon and Maya's visit. Besides, it's less than a week. How bad can it get?

Two

Saturday, May 4

"I'm taking you girls shopping," my aunt announced this morning as I poured myself a cup of coffee and percolated on a plan that might allow me to escape my relatives today.

Maya groaned, and I made what I thought was a polite yet insistent protest, but Shannon was not to be deterred.

"No arguing," she said to Maya, then looked at me. "Can you drive us, Kim?"

"I, uh, I guess so."

"It's settled. Let's leave around noon."

I thought we were going to the local mall, but Shannon insisted we drive to the city. "We need the good shops."

"Yeah, right," muttered Maya from the backseat.

Then Shannon continued to talk, about a mile a

minute, about what we would look for, what was hot, what was not, and I mostly just blanked it all out. I mean, who cares really? I'm sure that I don't.

But I reassured myself, in four days they'd be gone. And tonight I would go to youth group, tomorrow to church, and on Monday I planned to return to school after a week off. I would've gone back sooner, but Dad really thought I needed to be home. I have no idea why since it's driven me nearly nuts hanging with these two freaks, but at least there's an end in sight.

Once we were in the city, I managed to convince Shannon that the new mall there was pretty good. "They have lots of designer shops," I told her, rattling off a few names as if I knew what I was talking about. I didn't mention that parking there was less of a nightmare than downtown, and finally we were there, walking around the busy, noisy mall like the strangest threesome ever.

Shannon, leading the way, reminded me of a mechanized Barbie doll that someone had wound up too tightly. She wore bright-colored capri pants and a top that was a couple sizes too small, and her highly styled blond hair literally bobbed up and down with each quick step. But how she managed to stay upright on those tall spike heels was a complete mystery to me.

Maya, on the other hand, looked like a sedated earth muffin as she slowly shuffled along, a couple steps behind us, in her weird flat sandals that made her feet look like flippers. She had on this faded tie-dyed dress that reached nearly to her ankles and looked like something literally left over from the sixties. But despite her dreary outfit, her face was still stunningly beautiful—and she appeared almost goddesslike in the way she held up her head.

And there I was, with my short black hair and my distinctly Korean features, looking like a midget next to these two tall females. Not particularly caring about appearances, I still had on my morning frump outfit of baggy khakis, pale blue T-shirt, and well-worn flip-flops.

Shannon seemed like a driven person as she dragged us from shop to shop, forcing us to search through the racks and try things on. Well, mostly me since Maya usually refused, complaining that her mom's taste was tasteless and tacky. But I was trying to be a good sport, for Mom's sake, and for the sake of peace and sanity. It seemed that Shannon was determined to shop and to spend money, buying lots of stuff—for all three of us.

"Is she always like this?" I finally asked Maya as we waited for Shannon to pay for her last purchases and rejoin us out in the mall.

"Just when she's high."

"High?" I studied Maya's blasé expression. Was she serious?

She just shrugged. "You know."

Now it would've been easy to just let it go, but for some reason I couldn't. Call it just plain curiosity, but I wanted to know. "No," I told Maya. "I don't know. Do you mean high as in high on something?"

Maya gave me that look—the one where she appears to be the all-knowing adult and I am the stupid child, even though I'm two years older than she is. "What do you think?"

"I don't know what to think," I said in frustration. "But it sounds like you're saying that your mom is high on something."

"Duh."

But now Shannon was approaching, loaded down with more bags, but still looking like she could break world records in a shopathon—if there was such a thing.

"Oh, there's a Versace shop." She pointed to a sign down the way.

"I've had enough," announced Maya. "And I'm hungry." She looked at me, I assume for support.

"I'm hungry too," I said.

"You can shop when we go home," Maya told her mom. "We've had enough."

Shannon looked disappointed, but to my surprise and relief she didn't argue. "Okay, let's get lunch. But not here. I want to go someplace nice. Do you know of anything, Kim?"

"Nice?"

"You know, something with good food and good service, hopefully something light. You know, California cuisine."

Well, I wasn't so sure, but I decided to take them to a restaurant I'd seen that wasn't far from the mall. And while I'm sure it wasn't exactly what Shannon had in mind, I thought it was okay. And fortunately for Maya's sake, they had vegetarian dishes too.

After we placed our orders, Shannon dominated the conversation. Not that either Maya or I cared since we were both being pretty quiet. But once Shannon started talking about childhood memories, some including my mom, my ears perked up.

"Everything was so boring when we were growing up," she said. "Our parents and community were so conservative, so uncreative…so white bread, you know, that I could hardly stand it." She looked at me. "But Patty didn't seem to mind. She actually fit in pretty well." Shannon laughed now. "Come to think of it, she chose something like that as an adult too."

I frowned. Was Shannon making fun of my mom?

"But I can see it was different for her," Shannon said quickly. "I mean, from what I can tell, your parents had a real nice marriage, Kim. Nothing like what we grew up with."

"Your parents weren't happily married?" Now this was news to me. Not that Mom had ever said otherwise. Come to think of it, she hadn't said much about her parents.

Shannon laughed. "The only reason our parents stayed married was because our mom was too insecure to make it on her own. But the way Dad treated her…" She just shook her head. "If she hadn't gotten sick, I'm sure she would've left him eventually. Maybe after us kids were grown."

"Oh."

"He never hit her, well, not that I ever knew of, but he could just cut her down with his words. Nothing she did was ever good enough." Then using some colorful and rather profane language, she described her father as someone I'm just as glad never to have met.

"Sounds familiar," Maya said in that bored-sounding voice.

"What?" demanded Shannon. "What do you mean?"

And that's when they got into it—right there in this relatively nice restaurant where, thankfully, I didn't know a single soul. Maya started yelling at her mother, saying how horribly Shannon had treated both Maya and Nick…and that's when I quietly excused myself to the ladies' restroom, where I sought refuge for about ten minutes or so.

When I emerged from the restroom, it sounded quieter, and I hoped that meant the fireworks were over. But when I returned to the table I could see that they were both smoldering, and it would only be a matter of time before the explosives came out again.

Fortunately, or not (depending on your perspective) they saved their nastiest arguments for the way home. I tried to tune them out as I drove, reminding myself that I should just focus on driving, but it was hard to ignore everything—the meanness, the bitterness, the knife-sharp jabs going back and forth. And I remembered what Maya had said back at the mall about Shannon being "high." And I wondered if that might really be true. And if so, perhaps it had something to do with all their problems.

Because while Maya wasn't completely innocent, it did seem like Shannon was doing a pretty poor job of mothering. And maybe if she handled things differently, well, perhaps it would be better for Maya. But then who can know for sure? Besides God, that is.

And so as I drove, I just silently prayed for both of them. But mostly for Maya. I think I was starting to feel sorry for her.

After we got home, Shannon announced that she was going to cook dinner tonight. I tried to tell her that wasn't really necessary, since people from both churches (mine and my parents) had been dropping off food all week. Our refrigerator was already packed. But Shannon insisted.

"You guys need some good healthy food. All these fat-laden casseroles are going to clog your arteries and kill you."

I didn't mention that I had hardly been eating anything anyway. Or that my dad seems to have lost his appetite as well. Besides, I figured it would keep Shannon busy for a couple of hours or so. And when she asked to borrow Mom's car to go to the store, I couldn't really think of any reason to say no. I just hoped she wouldn't get into a wreck.

The house was a lot quieter with Shannon gone. Maya was reading a magazine she'd picked up at the mall. It looked like some kind of environmentalist political kind of thing. Not exactly my cup of tea.

Not that I don't care about the environment. I do. But not in the impassioned way Maya does. And certainly not at the moment when it's all I can do to keep from falling apart. But the whole "save the earth" thing is one of Maya's hot buttons, and one that Shannon likes to push when she needs to get a rise out of her daughter.

So while things were relatively calm, I went to my room to practice violin, and work on some homework as well as my column. But it was strange as I played violin; it's like I could feel someone listening to me. I paused for a moment and checked to see if perhaps Maya was standing outside my door, but no one was there. Then I played some more and still had that feeling. Suddenly I wondered if it could be my mom. So I played for about an hour until my fingers, which were a little out of shape, began to get sore. And now I'm thinking maybe she can hear me. As a result, I think I'll be practicing more regularly again.

After my homework (which Nat dropped by yesterday) was finished, I decided to tackle a real letter in my column. Dad told me that I could take a hiatus (that's like a break), but I was worried that if Just Ask Jamie's column stopped at exactly the same time my mom died…well, someone might begin to suspect. And as lame as it sounds to be writing an anonymous teen advice column, I've gotten rather used to it and find a weird kind of comfort in doing it. Besides, the extra money's not bad either. It figured that the first one I'd pull out had to do with moms and daughters. Oh, well.

Dear Jamie,

I am a reasonably responsible sixteen-year-old. I have a driver's license, a part-time job, and my own car that I bought myself. I also pay my own insurance and get decent grades. I don't drink or do drugs. Even so, my mom doesn't trust me, and she treats me like an eight-year-old. She's always checking up on me, she doesn't let me go out on weeknights, and she gives me a really early curfew on weekends. She doesn't like my friends and says they're a bad influence, which is totally not true. I'd go live with my dad, except that it's too far away, and I like my school. I'm seriously considering trying to get my own place. What should I do?

Desperate Daughter

Dear Desperate,

Based on what you've told me, it does sound like your mom is being a little overprotective. Of course, that's probably just because she loves you. Still, I think she'd be smart to lighten up. It's too bad she can't see what a great daughter she's raised. Instead of being on your case, she should be proud of you. Why don't you show her my response and see what she has to say about it. And tell her that I congratulate her for having such a fine daughter. Good luck!

Just Jamie

Okay, I was tempted to add something like, "and you should be thankful you have a mother who's still alive and who still cares about you," but that might make someone guess about Jamie's true identity. I have to be careful.

Anyway, after finishing up a couple more letters for the column, I decided to see how Shannon's dinner was going, maybe even offer to help. But when I saw Mom's kitchen looking as if a pipe bomb had just gone off, it was all I could do to slip away without totally losing it. My mom's neat and orderly kitchen was blown apart, completely wrecked in just one afternoon! And to think I was worried about her car!

Three

Sunday, May 5

I went to youth group last night. I even invited Maya to
go with me, but she just made fun of the idea. And in all
fairness, I would've done the same thing at her age. In
fact, I'm sure I did just less than a year ago…back when
Natalie was always trying to get me to go to hers. She's
not doing that anymore. The sad truth is, she's not even
going at all. Okay, I know she's still bummed about Ben,
but she needs to move on. Last week, she told me that
she's agreed to go see the counselor, but I'm not
convinced she's sincere. My guess is that she's just trying
to put on a good act for me, since Mom died. Like she
thinks it will make things better for me if she's getting
help. Come to think of it, it wouldn't hurt. But I have my
doubts that she'll follow through. So far she hasn't.

And I can tell she's still depressed. Oh, she tries to act
as if she's not, especially when she's trying to "encourage"

me. But I can see right through her. And instead of feeling better after her little "pep talks," I feel more depressed than before. But I can't tell her this. I mean, at least she's trying, right?

I guess I'm just feeling pretty bummed tonight. And going to youth group did not bolster my spirits one bit. Maybe it's just me. Or maybe things are changing. I'm not sure. But for starters, Josh had someone else give the message tonight, and it was pretty lame, or at least I thought so. And Cesar wasn't there, so I didn't even have someone to review it with afterward. Usually Cesar and I see eye to eye on most things, and when we don't, it can be a pretty interesting discussion. Anyway, the whole evening was pretty much a letdown.

Oh, I don't know what I really expected, but sometimes it's so cool to be there, and I feel so much at home. And I guess I thought, well, especially after losing Mom...that I'd get some kind of encouragement.

As a result I probably seemed a little moodier than usual when I got home. I walked right past where Shannon and Maya were sitting in front of the TV without even saying "hey" and headed straight to the kitchen. And of course, Maya jumped right onto this.

"So your little youth group didn't cheer you up tonight?" she said when she found me standing in front of the window of the dark kitchen, a can of unopened soda in my hand.

Without turning, I told her that it wasn't their job to cheer me up.

"Then why do you go?" She pulled up a chair, as if I'd invited her to join me.

Okay, normally on a good day, I might see this as an opportunity to share my faith, but this wasn't exactly a good day. To be honest, I had no desire to have a conversation with this girl. So I said nothing.

"Oh, I get it," she said. "You go because it's the right thing to do. I know people like that. They do all kinds of crud they don't enjoy, but it's the RIGHT thing to do. So without questioning and acting like preprogrammed robots, off they go just so they—"

"That's not how it is." I turned to look at her. Okay, I wish I'd taken just a split second to pray—to ask God to help me say something helpful or enlightening or even kind. But I did not.

"How is it then?"

"I go because I want to go."

She smiled and nodded. "Yeah, I get that too. Some people get this weird kind of pleasure when they do things they don't enjoy. Is it like that for you?"

"No." The impatience in my voice must've been obvious. "It's not."

"So what then?"

I shook my head. "I guess it's a personal thing, Maya. Maybe someday when you're older you'll understand." Then I took my soda and went up to my room. And naturally, once I was up there I felt bad. So ungracious. So unkind. So unlike my mother. I think I am a total failure.

Wednesday, May 8

It was a relief to return to school this week. A kind of
mind-numbing relief of being in my element, my
comfort zone, where I could go through the paces and
perform with perfection without hardly even trying. The
only times I got uncomfortable were when someone
offered me sympathy for losing my mom. I could've
done without that. Still, after the first day, I managed to
come up with some pat responses that made these
moments pass more smoothly.

"Kim," someone would say, "I'm so sorry to hear
about your mom. Are you doing okay?"

To which I'd respond. "Yes, I'm sorry too. I
appreciate your concern. Thanks." And somehow that
just stopped it all right there. No more explaining or
hugging or tears. A relief to me, because I just don't think
I can take much more.

And going to school provided a nice escape from my
relatives too. At least during the day. After that, I get
pushed to my limits every night. Shannon really believes
that she can cook now. But just like before, she makes
these big horrible messes and skanky food that no one,
even someone starving, would want to eat. And I end
up cleaning it all up.

Last night, as I was scrubbing down the stove
Shannon had turned into a grease pit, enjoying a bit of
solitude since no one besides Dad (and I always tell him
no) offers to help me, I felt somewhat reassured that at
least it would be the last time for this kind of KP.

Shannon and Maya would be leaving the next morning. So I was in a little bit better spirits.

It even occurred to me that I'd probably found a tiny bit of solace while working so hard to put Mom's kitchen back in order every night. In a way, it was like a small connection to her. Almost like when I'm practicing violin. So I suppose I should've been thankful for Shannon's "cooking efforts."

Just as I was finishing up, Maya made an appearance. "Need any help?"

I kind of laughed. "Good timing. I'm just about done."

"Oh." Now she actually looked slightly disappointed. "Sorry."

"Here." I handed her a sponge. "You can wipe down the microwave if you want."

So she did it. I finished up the sink, and then we really were done. "Thanks," I told her.

"Yeah, right. Big deal."

I wasn't sure how to respond. "So...are you guys all ready to go? Dad said you have an early flight in the morning."

She shrugged. "Yeah. I'm ready, but then I travel light. Don't know about Mom. She just went up to start packing. I'm guessing she'll be up past midnight, but knowing her, she might stay up all night anyway. Hope she hasn't disturbed you guys, although I'm sure you've noticed by now she's kind of a night owl."

I nodded without mentioning that Shannon has, in

fact, woken me several times, or how Dad and I would both be relieved to see our guests leaving tomorrow. No need to be rude. "It does make me curious though…"

"About what?"

"Well, I know you're homeschooled, but if Shannon stays up all night and it seems like she sleeps a lot during the day, how do you do homeschool?"

Maya just laughed. "Oh, I have my books and my computer and the assignments I get online. And if I'm in the mood, I sometimes get them done."

"But what if you're not? In the mood I mean?"

"Then I get behind."

"So, are you? Behind?"

"Yeah, you could say that."

"Does Shannon know?"

Maya shrugged. "She doesn't pay much attention."

"Maya?" I began, knowing that I was getting onto shaky ground. "Is it true what you said about her, that time you said she was high? Was she really on something?"

She smirked then said, "Well, yeah," like she was stating the obvious.

"Does she take a prescription? Like antidepressants?"

"Not exactly a prescription," she said, "But something like that. It's her own little formula. Some are from various doctors. Some are from the street. Whatever it takes to keep Shannon going, Shannon will take."

"So is she like an addict?"

Maya threw back her head and laughed.

"I take that as a yes."

Sobering, Maya nodded. "Yeah, Shannon's an addict."

"Has she ever gotten help?"

"Help?" Maya looked slightly puzzled. "You mean like rehab or counseling?"

"Yeah, some form of addiction therapy."

"Well, according to the research I did a while ago, back when I was young enough to think things could change, I heard that an addict can't be helped until she admits she has a problem."

"And your mom hasn't done that?"

Maya firmly shook her head. "No way. Shannon thinks that Shannon is perfectly fine. It's the rest of the world that's messed up."

I sighed and actually put my hand on her shoulder. "I'm sorry, Maya."

And to my surprise this simple gesture seemed to touch her, and she even got tears in her eyes, but she didn't say anything.

"If there's ever anything we can do," I continued, not even knowing why, "please, let us know. I mean, we are your family after all."

And so we agreed to stay in contact via e-mail. And then I even hugged her. "You are my only cousin," I told her with actual tears in my eyes. "And while we may not be related by blood or genetics, we are related by mothers, and I know my mother would want to help you—if it's at all possible.

And now that they're gone—Dad said he took them to the airport in plenty of time for their early flight—I am even more certain of this. If Mom were here, she would do whatever it took to help Maya. And of course, she'd want to help Shannon too. That's just how she was.

Not that it would be easy to help Shannon, since I've heard the same thing about addicts that Maya heard. I do think it's true that they have to want help, and they usually don't. But I told Maya I'd be praying for Shannon to wake up and figure things out.

Of course, I didn't tell Maya that I'd be praying for her too. That might've overwhelmed her and been enough to intimidate her and keep her from e-mailing me. And for some reason, I think this communication link may be important.

So as much as I've blown it with Shannon and Maya this past week, this is one thing I might've done right— reaching out to Maya. And I think maybe Mom would be happy with it. Of course, I'm sure she'd be sad to find out that her little sister is a drug addict. Or maybe she'd had suspicions all along. Anyway, she must know these things by now. It's not like there are secrets in heaven, are there?

It's probably because of that conversation with Maya that I decided to answer a couple of letters about addiction tonight. And I'm thinking that when the paper comes out, I'll forward them to Maya, pretending like, "hey, look at this." And who knows? It might help.

Dear Jamie,

I think my mom has a gambling problem, and I don't know what to do about it. She used to play bingo all the time, and that was bad enough, but now she's been driving out to this casino during the day while no one's at home. I caught her coming home one time, and she was so happy (because she'd won) that she gave me some money and swore me to secrecy. The problem is that our family is going through some tough financial times (Mom handles our money), and my dad has no idea that she's gambling. What should I do?

High Roller's Kid

Dear Kid,

It sounds like you could be onto something. I would suggest you talk directly to your mom. 1) Tell her your suspicions and that you think she needs help. 2) Ask her to come clean to your dad ASAP. 3) If she refuses, tell her that you're going to speak to your dad. It's not fair for your mom's addiction to drag down your whole family. It'll be tough, at first, but later on she will probably thank you for it. Hang in there!

Just Jamie

I'm thinking a gambling addiction couldn't be as harmful as drugs. I know it's bad and that it can bring financial ruin on a family, but drugs can literally kill. The next letter has to do with just that. It came right after

Mom died, and the subject was so heavy I just couldn't force myself to answer it. Today I will.

Dear Jamie,

You're the only one I can tell this secret to. But I have to tell someone. I'm twelve, and I have two younger brothers who I help to take care of. My parents manufacture meth drugs in our house. They've done it for as long as I can remember. Sometimes they even make me help them. We always have plenty of money since business is pretty good. But lately I've been really scared. I know my parents are messed up, but I think our whole family is a mess too. Also, I'm worried that I'll end up jail if I tell, since I've helped them. Please, tell me what to do.

Over Her Head

Dear Over,

I'm so glad you wrote. You are absolutely right—you do need to talk to someone. Right away! Is there an adult in your life who you can trust? Like a grandparent or pastor or teacher or counselor? You need to go to that person and tell him or her what's going on now. Manufacturing meth isn't just illegal, it's <u>extremely dangerous</u>. There could be a fire or an explosion or serious chemical poisoning that could hurt you or your little brothers. You kids need to get out of that house as soon as possible. But you will need a responsible adult to help you through this mess. And no, you do not need to worry about getting in trouble. You are the victim here. If nothing else, you could go directly to the police. Just make sure you do something. And do it today!

Just Jamie

Now I'm feeling seriously guilty that I didn't answer this sooner. Those poor kids! What was I thinking? I will definitely be praying for them—with all my heart. What kind of parents act like this anyway? Putting themselves and their children at such huge risk? Oh, yeah, ones like my aunt. But then she doesn't actually cook dope in her home—at least I don't think so. Maya didn't mention anything like this.

Anyway, I plan to show Dad this pitiful letter tomorrow, and I'm hoping he can keep an eye on the news and keep me informed if there's a bust that fits the description of Over Her Head's stupid parents. And while I'm on the subject with Dad, I plan to tell him about Shannon and her little problems too.

Man, life can be so sad sometimes.

Four

Friday, May 10

As much as I hated having Shannon and Maya here with all their yelling and cursing and bickering, I have to say that I almost miss it now that they're gone. Our house is so freaky quiet that sometimes I feel like I'm going to scream, just so I can hear some noise. Oh, it's not as if it was really noisy while Mom was alive, but there were sounds...comforting sounds I miss.

Like the way she'd have the morning news show playing on her little kitchen TV while she tried to talk me into having something for breakfast, or the public radio station she sometimes listened to in the afternoon, or just the sound of her working in the kitchen, sometimes humming to herself if she didn't know anyone was listening. But now I come home from school, and it's perfectly still and quiet. And even though it's May, it feels cold to me too. Like our house is dead.

I tried playing my violin for a while today, but the sound of it echoing throughout the silent house just got to me—it was so lonely and desperate sounding that I had to stop. I put it away and closed the case and just wandered around until I came to my parents' room.

Then I went inside and just looked around. Dad hasn't really changed anything yet. Shannon kept telling him that the sooner he got rid of Mom's stuff, the sooner he'd be able to move on with his life. But I don't think he wants to move on. Not like that anyway. Neither do I, for that matter. So I just stood there and looked and smelled and absorbed what little bits of my mother still remained.

Finally, I went into her closet and leaned into her clothes, breathing in the air that once surrounded her. Then I closed the door and sat down, right there amid her shoes. And holding her bathrobe in my arms, I just cried and cried.

I'm not sure how long I stayed in her closet, but I finally got worried that Dad might come home and freak out to find me in there like that, so I left. But I promised myself that I would come back and do it again if I need to. And I took her bathrobe to my room. I know it's childish, but I just can't help myself.

I've been trying to make dinner for Dad and me the past couple of nights, but neither of us seems to have much appetite these days. Whether it's due to my less-than-polished cooking skills or missing Mom, I'm not sure. But tonight, Dad opted for takeout. I offered to pick it up, but he said he had to pick up something anyway.

I wanted to ask him if I could come along, just for the company and also because I didn't want to be home alone again, but I could tell that he wanted to be alone. Still, it worries me that he's alone too much. He's so quiet about everything lately. I just really wanted to talk to him.

So I decided to do what Mom used to do when Dad brought home takeout. She'd go ahead and set the table and make it look nice, just like a regular dinner. Maybe that would make Dad feel more at home and he'd want to sit around and talk. I even made a pot of tea since Dad was bringing home Chinese.

But when he got back and sat down, it was just the same. We both ate in silence. Oh, I tried to bring up some things. I asked a couple of questions about the column and the newspaper, but I could tell he had no interest in really talking. And I know it's because he's hurting. But it hurts me too.

When Matthew called to see whether or not I wanted to go out tonight—since I'd told him I wasn't too sure earlier—I said, "Why not?" I didn't add, "Since Dad won't talk to me anyway." But that's how I felt as I cleaned up the kitchen and watched my dad hiding behind his "Newsweek" magazine in the family room.

For the most part, Matthew has been being very considerate of my feelings lately. I know the whole thing with my mom is pretty unsettling to him, and he's not quite sure how to handle it. But at least he lets me vent if

I need to. And tonight I needed to. Especially after the movie we saw.

It was an Italian film with subtitles, and it started out pretty good. Matthew had heard it was amazing. But what he didn't realize was that it was about World War II and lots and lots of death. Just what I needed. By the time the flick was over, my head hurt from crying so much. Then we went out for coffee, and I really laid into him.

"Why that movie?" I demanded. Then, of course, he told me that he was as surprised as I was. But I carried on for a while, and he just sat there and took it. Finally, he reached for my hand and said he was sorry. And I could tell that he really was.

"No, I'm the one who should be sorry," I said. "I'm making this into a great big deal. I know you didn't mean for it to be like this. I'm sorry."

And so we were okay. And maybe it was a good thing after all. Maybe I really did need to watch other people in pain. Maybe I did need to be reminded that I'm not the only one who's lost a loved one. And maybe I needed to cry again. So when it was all said and done, I guess I felt a teeny bit better. But as Matthew drove me home, I could tell he was feeling down.

"I'm sorry," I said again, suddenly feeling guilty. "Are you feeling bad because of me? I really shouldn't have gotten so wigged out about that movie. I mean, now that I think about it, it was pretty good."

"No…" he said slowly. "That's not really it."

"What is it then?"

"I'm not sure. Maybe it's just a bunch of things."

"Like what?" I persisted.

He shrugged. "You've got enough on your plate, Kim. I don't want to dump on you. Besides, it's small stuff compared to what you've been dealing with."

"Really, Matthew, I want to know," I said in my most persuasive voice. "If something's bugging you, you should be able to tell me."

He smiled now. "Yeah. But not tonight, okay? I think you've had enough emotion for one night."

"You mean it's something emotional?"

He kind of laughed. "Not exactly. Let's just chill for now. Okay?"

I said, "Okay," but underneath I really wanted to know what was getting to him. And suddenly I worried that it might have something to do with our relationship. Naturally, I went to the worst-case scenario. Did Matthew want to break up with me?

Finally we were at my house, and as usual, he walked me to the door, bending down to give me a little peck before he said, "Good night." But as I went into the house, I was feeling even more certain that something between us was wrong. I really believed he was going to break up with me. That had to be it. But the idea of this sliced through me like a knife.

Dad had already gone to bed. Not that I would've discussed this with him. At least I didn't think so. But I suppose I did want to talk to someone. I considered calling Natalie, but it was pretty late, and besides she's still so bummed about her own life. So I went to my room and just sat down and thought about how things have been with Matthew and me. And now it seems more obvious than ever. I'm surprised I didn't see this coming.

Our relationship has been pretty minimal for the past few weeks. Maybe even the last couple of months. But then what could you expect? When your mom is sick and dying—of course you're going to be pre-occupied with that. I probably tried to pretend like everything was fine, and there was even a time when I thought Mom was better and that God was healing her. But I'm sure that Matthew sensed I was distracted. How could I not be?

Even prom, which was surprisingly fun, was overshadowed with Mom's health. And then she died that very same night. So naturally I haven't been giving Matthew much attention. And this is his senior year, and his goal had been to have a good time. But then he hooked up with me. No wonder he's ready to dump me.

But he's such a nice guy. I'm sure he's been postponing this breakup because of everything that's gone on lately. I mean, you don't break up with a girl right after her mom dies—unless you're a jerk. And Matthew is not a jerk.

So I decided to IM him, hoping he'd be home by now and possibly online. But he's not. Of course, I didn't mention my concern about breaking up. I just said, "hey, are you there?" But when he didn't answer, I signed off. And even though I'm trying to let it go, trying to pretend that I don't suspect what I do, I have a feeling I'm right on target. I am certain that Matthew, my first real boyfriend, is ready to move on—and it's killing me.

And so in my usual distraction mode, I attacked some column letters. Maybe reading about someone else's heartache would cheer me up. And believe me, there's plenty of it. The number one topic teens write to me about has to do with romance gone badly. Usually, I skipped most of those letters, but tonight I was ready.

Dear Jamie,

There's a certain guy who I've been really good friends with for about a year now. We hang together a lot, and he's been like my very best friend. He's so easy to get along with, and I can tell him almost anything. I guess I've known for a while that I have kind of a crush on him. But I have never let on. I always act like we're just friends. And that's mostly cool since I get to be around him so much. Until last week. That's when he told me that he likes this girl, I mean, like he's totally into her. And he wants me to see if she's into him. He even thought maybe I could talk to her. And this whole thing is making me crazy. I really want to tell him how much I like him, but I'm afraid that will ruin everything. What should I do?

Just Friends

Dear Just,

It must be hard to be in that position. But you need to accept that you put yourself in it. First of all, you haven't been totally honest with this guy. You're acting like you are "just friends" when you actually really like him. Isn't that a little deceptive? I mean, friends are open with each other, telling secrets and stuff, and he's been open with you. But you sort of took advantage of it by pretending to be "just friends." I think it's mostly your own fault that you got hurt, and now you have two choices: 1) You can let things continue as they've been, deceiving him and hurting yourself, or 2) you can tell him the truth and put your friendship at risk. I recommend the second option because at least it shouldn't hurt for as long. And after this I suggest you be honest in any relationship that's important to you.

Just Jamie

Okay, that's probably not the kindest response I've written. Maybe Jamie is feeling cranky tonight. Let's see if I can do better on the next one.

Dear Jamie,

My parents wouldn't let me date until I was seventeen, which seemed totally unfair since all my friends were already dating long before that. But then "John" transferred to my school shortly after my seventeenth birthday, and I thought maybe my parents weren't so lame after all. Anyway John and I have been going together since Christmas, and he is the coolest guy I've even known. I love him with all my heart. And up until last week, I thought he loved me too. But then he broke up with me. Just like that. He says he likes someone else. I am totally devastated. I know my heart is broken into about a million pieces. I don't think I'll ever get over this. I wish I could die. What should I do?

Shattered Girl

Dear Shattered,

I know it must feel like the end of your world, but trust me, it's not. Even so, it's got to feel really, really rotten. I wish I could say that time heals all wounds, but I'm not sure that's true. I think the only thing you can do is to just keep going, working your way through this pain until you reach the place where it doesn't hurt so much. I recommend that you reach out to God during this time—He's a great comforter when your heart is broken. Heartache, like grief, will probably have various stages (like denial, anger, depression...), but if you work through these things, you should finally get to a place of acceptance. In the meantime, don't isolate yourself. Spend time with good friends and do things you once enjoyed. Hopefully the shadows will pass. And next time, you'll be more careful before you give your heart away.

Just Jamie

I know I should be preparing myself to take this advice too. Because I still have the strongest feeling that Matthew is ready to call it quits. But before I turned off my computer for the night, I decided to just e-mail him. Why not take Jamie's advice and "just be honest"? Why not just ask? And so I do. I don't go into much detail, only that I'm concerned he wants to break up and feels uncomfortable about it. But I assure him that he can talk to me—that it's okay. I just hope I can be as strong as I am trying to appear. God help me. I will be praying myself to sleep tonight.

Five

Sunday, May 12

As it turned out, Matthew had no intention of breaking up with me. Or so he assured me last night. He'd spent most of the day doing yard work at his grandparents' house and hadn't even seen my e-mail until he got home later in the afternoon. Worried that I might be sitting around freaking, he called me as soon as he read it.

"We need to talk," he said.

Oh, no, I was thinking, here it comes. "Yeah?"

"Can we do something tonight?"

Well, I'd actually been thinking about going to youth group, but I quickly ditched that plan, figuring it was more important to take care of this. And if I was about to get my heart broken, I'd prefer to do it on the weekend and in privacy if possible. So I agreed.

"I'll pick you up at seven," he said. And then we hung up. Of course, that left me feeling pretty antsy. As a result, I paced around the house like a caged tiger. Dad was doing something on his computer in his den, and I could tell he didn't want to be disturbed. Whether he was actually working or what, I wasn't sure. But as I slowly walked past the open door, I could tell by the serious tilt of his head and the way he focused on his screen that he wasn't in a talking mode. Not that I would've really wanted to talk to him, at least not about Matthew. That would be weird.

Suddenly, I just couldn't take it anymore. I had to call Nat. Okay, I knew she was still acting all weird and sad about Benjamin and the breakup, but this could prove a good distraction for her, might even remind her she wasn't the only one with problems. Besides, Christians are supposed to support each other during hard times, right? Well, I was on hard times.

"I need to talk," I said shortly after she answered.

"What's wrong?" she asked with what sounded like mild interest.

"Can you come over?"

But as usual, she was watching Krissy and Micah, so I went over to her house. Actually, this was a relief. I get so tired of the silence at my house that even her bickering siblings sound good to my ears. At least for a while.

Finally, we were up in her room, which to my surprise looked pretty disgusting. "What happened in here?" I removed what appeared to be dirty laundry in order to sit on her chair.

"Huh?" She looked around blankly, as if she didn't notice the change. Natalie used to be something of a neat freak. One of the things we used to have in common, although I was always more obsessive about it. She used to brag on how her room was the cleanest place in their whole house. And up until now that had been true.

And she used to take more care with her appearance too. But her shoulder-length blond hair was ratty and in need of a wash. And although my willowy friend usually looks good in anything, those nasty-looking sweats were really pushing it.

"Never mind," I said, pretending not to notice the piles of clothes and clutter or even the disgusting bowl of what might've once been Fruit Loops. Unless those spots of color were something alive and growing—a science experiment perhaps.

She flopped down on her unmade bed and just looked at me. "What's up?"

So I told her my theory about Matthew, how I was certain he was about to break up, and how I needed to talk.

"So…" She just shrugged, like no big deal.

"So?" That was the best she could do?

"Yeah. So he's going to break up, Kim. It happens."

I felt myself tensing up. I mean, when Ben broke up with Nat, she totally fell apart. I listened to her ranting and raving for hours—and that was during the time when my mom was dying. I probably wasted precious time listening to Natalie obsessing over Ben when I could've been with my mom. The very idea of this made me feel like I was about to start crying.

"I know it's tough, Kim," she said in a flat-sounding voice, not the least bit compassionate sounding, "but you have to get over it, move on." She narrowed her eyes, just a tiny bit. "Isn't that what you told me?"

"Well, maybe…" I wanted to leave now. "I can't remember exactly."

"But it hurts, doesn't it?"

I nodded, a big lump growing in my throat. Still, I was thinking it's not the getting dumped part that hurt so much—at least not yet. But it's this apathetic attitude of my supposedly best friend that hurts. That and knowing I really don't have anyone to talk to anymore. Not my mom, not Nat, and before long, not Matthew as well. It was pretty dismaying.

"Thanks for the pep talk," I said as I stood up.

"Hey, I'm just telling it like it is."

"Right." But I turned away and reached for the door. All I wanted was to get away from her. If I wasn't mistaken, I think she was actually enjoying my agony over Matthew. Okay, maybe it was just a case of "misery loves company." I'm not sure, but it felt lousy. And I'd had enough.

I fretted around the house for a while, doing a couple of chores. And then, I think as a result of seeing Natalie's sorry room, I decided that mine could use a little help, so I spent about an hour tidying up. And I had to admit that made me feel just a teeny bit better. Then I spent some time getting dressed, trying on about six outfits before I found one that seemed right. I mean, if I'm going to be dumped, I'd like to go down looking good.

Finally it was nearly seven, and I went out to the kitchen to wait.

"Going out tonight?" my dad asked. Was that relief I heard in his voice? Was he glad to have me out of the house so he could be completely alone? And if so, what was up with that?

"Yeah."

"With Matthew?"

"Yeah."

"He's a nice kid."

"Yeah—" My voice kind of broke by the third "yeah."

My dad looked at me with a concerned expression. "He is, isn't he?"

I nodded, maybe a bit too vigorously. "Oh, yeah, he definitely is. Very nice."

"Are you okay, Kim?"

I glanced up at the kitchen clock. It was seven o'clock, and I knew Matthew would be here any second. No way did I want to break down into tears now. "I'm fine, Dad." I held my chin up to bolster my sagging spirits. "How about you?" I looked directly at him, thinking it was his turn to sit on the hot seat.

He forced a pathetic little smile. "I'm fine too, I guess."

And then I heard Matthew's pickup pulling into the driveway. But I just couldn't leave on such a lame note. So I threw my arms around Dad, hugged him, and said, "Yeah right, we're both perfectly fine. What a couple of big fat liars!"

He kind of laughed now. "Well, we're trying anyway."

"See ya."

And as I headed out, meeting Matthew halfway up the walk, I realized how fragile Dad and I still are. Maybe we should wear a warning label like: "Caution, contents under pressure—may explode at slightest provocation." Or maybe we should have a well-defined grieving period, like some cultures that require the bereaved to wear black or certain garments that remind everyone that they are still grieving.

I heard about a place in the South Pacific where the widow is draped in hundreds of long strands of seed necklaces so they cover her entire torso, and she's not allowed to remarry until all the seeds have withered or rotted away—and it could take years.

"Hey, Kim," Matthew says as we hug in front of my house. "You okay?"

I shrug, still trying to maintain some composure. "Yeah, I guess."

Then he opens the door and helps me into his truck. He's being so nice that it seems to confirm everything. He wants to dump me in a gentlemanly way. But I'd rather he just got it over with.

"It's so nice out that I thought we could go for a walk

or something," he says as he drives down the street.

Right. Go someplace private where no one can witness me falling apart when he shares the news. Whatever. I sit in silence as he drives. He's talking about all the yard work he did for his grandparents and how he aches in places he didn't even know he had. Finally, he pulls over by a park not too far from my house. Convenient, I'm thinking as I get out. If things get really bad, I can walk home.

We walk over to where a little pond and fountain are situated in the center of the park. On really hot days, the neighborhood kids like to come here to cool off. My mom never liked me to do that. She worried that the water wasn't chlorinated and that I'd come home with some horrible disease. But Nat and I sneaked over a few times and got into some good water fights, but then after I got home I would worry that I'd contracted some weird illness. Of course, I never did.

Matthew and I sit on a bench in front of the pond. A couple of kids are trying to sail a boat, but it keeps listing to one side, and I think it's about to go under.

"It's been a while since we've really talked," Matthew says in a somewhat serious tone. "And I know you've had a lot going on. But it's been two weeks since your mom died, and well, I was hoping—"

"Look," I say, interrupting what appears to be a carefully constructed speech. "Just cut to the chase, okay? You want to break up with me, and you're worried that I'm—"

"No, Kim, that's not it at all."

Now I'm a little stunned. "Really?"

"Really. I just needed to talk, okay?"

"Really?" I say again, feeling stupid.

"I mean it."

"You're certain?"

"Yeah. I was pretty surprised at your e-mail. Actually, I thought maybe you were kidding. Then I wondered if you wanted to break up with me." He frowns. "Do you?"

Okay, now I'm feeling a little confused. Is this some new kind of tactic—a way to gently break up with a girl who's just lost her mother? You make her think <u>she's</u> doing the breaking up?

He looks a little hurt. "Do you, Kim? Is this your way of letting me—?"

"No," I say quickly. "Not at all. But I just realized what a pathetic sort of girlfriend I've been these past couple of months. I mean, I'm either checked out, worried, distracted, or like last night, just losing it completely. Talk about your high-maintenance relationship."

He smiles. "Have you heard me complaining?"

I feel a wave of relief. "No. You've been totally great, Matthew. But if you don't want to break up, what do you want to talk about?"

He sighs. "I just need to talk to someone…someone who knows me…someone I can trust."

"Of course," I assure him. "I'm so here for you. What's up?"

Then he tells me about how he wanted to stick

around after graduation, work during the summer, and go to community college for a year while he continues with his art. "I thought maybe after a year, maybe I could save up some money and get into a decent design school. Plus I'd have a few of my requirements out of the way, you know?" He smiles at me. "And I'd still be around for my best girl."

I can't even describe how good this makes me feel. "That sounds like a cool plan to me. But then I could be a little biased."

He nods. "Maybe. Or maybe you just get me."

"So, what's the problem?"

"My grandparents."

"Oh." Now I know enough about Matthew to know that these are his paternal grandparents, and that even though his dad's been (shall I say?) a jerk, his grandparents have been very supportive of Matthew. Unfortunately they don't treat his mother with much respect, and this can be the source of conflict at times. Serious conflict.

"My grandpa wants me to go to his alma mater," Matthew continues his tale. "And last fall, I think just to appease him, I applied to go. Naturally, I figured my less-than-stellar grades would insure my rejection."

Matthew's grades, while not nearly as good as mine, aren't all that shabby either. He is, after all, in Honor Society.

As if reading my expression, he adds, "It's an Ivy League school."

"Oh."

"Anyway, I got my acceptance letter a few weeks ago."

"Really?" Now despite everything, I do think this is exciting. Matthew at an Ivy League school? Impressive!

"Yeah, I would've told you, but so much was going on. Besides, I wasn't even sure I wanted to consider it."

"But you are?"

He shrugs. "I don't know…"

I hear a kid yelling and look up to see that not only the boat, but one of the boys is now in the pond. But since it's only about a foot deep, I'm not worried that we'll need to practice any life-saving techniques.

"My grandpa is really putting pressure on me."

"I'll bet." I turn my attention back to Matthew. "I'm sure it would make him proud."

"But I think it would hurt my mom."

"Why?"

"Oh, you know…they're always at each other. She thinks he's an arrogant jerk, and he thinks she's an over-the-hill hippie." He kind of laughs.

"But I'd think your mom would be pleased to see you going to such an impressive school, Matthew. Your mom respects education."

"That's true. But she also resents my grandpa's influence."

"But it's not like he'd be going to school with you."

"I know." He shoves his fingers through his hair, and

I can tell he's really frustrated by this little family tug-of-war that has him in the middle.

"What do you want, Matthew?"

He shakes his head. "I'm not sure."

"I mean, if your mom and your grandparents had nothing to say about anything, what would you want?" I pause as he considers this. "What is best for you?"

"That's just it, Kim. I can see that either plan would be good. I mean, I pretty much get free tuition if I go to Grandpa's alma mater, but then I feel kind of like I'd owe him something. Besides that, he's not all that supportive of my art. But if I stick around here, I have to earn my tuition myself. And even though I'm hoping for a scholarship, it might not happen. What if I end up with nothing more than a couple of years of community college and a dead-end job?"

I frown. It's hard to imagine someone like Matthew not making an absolute success of his life, but then you never know. What would Jamie tell him?

"So you see they both have their pros and cons. The problem is, I need to make a decision soon. My grandpa already asked for an extension since I missed their first deadline. If he wasn't such good buddies with the dean, I wouldn't have a chance."

"It must be hard for you," I finally say.

He nods.

"But if I were in your shoes, I'd have a distinct advantage."

"And that would be?"

"God."

He gives me that look, like <u>here we go again</u>. Not that I'm constantly preaching at him—I definitely am not—but I do express my faith when I feel the urge. And I'm feeling the urge now. "You know, Matthew, it really makes a difference when you have God leading you. It takes off a whole lot of pressure."

"So I suppose you know exactly what you're doing for college and the rest of your life, for that matter."

"No, silly. But I have some ideas, and I'm putting them before God. I'm asking Him to show me which way to go, to open the doors that need to be opened, and to close the doors to places I don't need to go. It really does simplify things."

"For some people."

I nod. "I remember feeling like that too, and not all that long ago. But having God really does make a difference, Matthew. Someday you might want to give Him a try."

He's looking out across the pond now. I can't tell if I'm aggravating him, or if he's actually considering my words. But we both sit there for what seems like several minutes.

"Just the same," I finally say, "I'm going to be praying that God will show you which direction is best. Hope you don't mind."

He smiles. "I don't mind. But it might do as much good to try a Ouija board, or maybe I should get a Magic 8 Ball."

I gently slug him in the arm. "Yeah, right."

So here it is Sunday night, I've just finished my homework, and I'm thinking I should be relieved that Matthew and I didn't break up. And for the most part, I am. But I also feel a little frustrated, and I'm not even sure I can put my finger on why that is.

I suppose it has to do with Matthew's indecision about college and life in general—not to mention God. And okay, who knows if I'd be doing any better if I were in his shoes—if I had two sets of family pulling me in two totally different directions. But I do pray and then trust God to lead me. And I guess it bugs me that Matthew can't do that.

For the first time, I might be starting to experience what I've heard other Christians call being "unequally yoked," and I guess it bothers me. Still, I really like Matthew. And he's probably the best friend I have right now, at least the only one I can actually talk to—besides God, that is.

Although it seems we've mostly talked about his life, his confusion about college, and his family disagreements—at least for these past two days. And come to think of it, that's probably only fair since so much of our focus has been on me and my problems up until recently. Maybe it's just his turn to have my attention for a change. I guess I have been a little self-centered lately.

But like I told him, I am praying for him. Not only that God will direct his future, but also that He will get a hold of Matthew's heart. I just wish his heart was as open as the writer of this letter.

Dear Jamie,

You seem to mention God in your letters a lot. This is really new to me since no one in my family has ever been into religion. But the way you talk about God makes Him seem real. And I guess I'm wondering what I should do to find out more about God. I asked my mom if we were any religion, and she said that her parents had been Methodists, but they never went to church much, and that as far as she knew, my dad's family had never gone to church at all. So I got to wondering what kind of religion would I be? How do you figure this stuff out?

Lost and Looking

Dear L & L,

First of all, I think it's great that you're looking. That's what God wants from all of us. Because the Bible says <u>if we look for God, we will find Him</u>. And the Bible is a good place to start looking. But beyond that, you might consider trying out one of the local youth groups. Perhaps in a neighborhood church or something like Young Life or Campus Life, which are nondenominational (meaning everyone is welcome). The other thing you can do is to pray directly to God. Believe it or not, He's ready and waiting for you to speak to Him. So don't be afraid,

speak up and ask God to show you the way to Himself.
I know you won't be disappointed!

Just Jamie

Six

Wednesday, May 15

My life used to be so simple. It's funny that I didn't really appreciate it then. I guess we just take the good times for granted. I remember when my biggest challenge was deciding which elective to take in school. I used to obsess over it for weeks. Now it seems as if I'm constantly bombarded with stuff.

Take Natalie. I wish someone would! Okay, that's not very kind or Christlike. But man, I have just about maxed out on her mood swings. I almost liked her better as Ghost Girl. Now you don't know what to expect. She can be callous and removed like the time I wanted some sympathy regarding Matthew. Or she can get angry over nothing—kind of like a time bomb, you never know when it's going to go off. Or she can be downright mean like she was today.

Now I know Natalie doesn't really like Marissa, but I thought she'd moved past her judgmental phase and had been trying to love her like Jesus would do. At least that's what Natalie told me several months ago when she was still on top of things. However, I'm not too sure that Nat even considers herself a Christian anymore. So I guess the rules have changed. And maybe I shouldn't have been surprised when the two of them got into it at lunch today. In all fairness, Marissa did push Nat's buttons. But it was still pretty embarrassing when Nat totally lost it with her.

It all starts when Marissa and Robert decide to make out at the lunch table. Unfortunately this isn't that unusual, and despite the fact that none of us really care for it, I guess they just can't help themselves. Yeah, right. Normally we make a couple of aggravated comments and then just try to ignore them as we carry on our own conversation. But for some reason, Natalie will not let it go today.

"Get a room," she says (not a terribly clever line) when she first notices them sucking on each other's faces.

Naturally, they ignore her.

"I mean it," she continues in a sharp tone. "You guys are grossing us out. Can't you take it outside?"

Still they ignore her. Or if anything Marissa starts really going at it. I'm surprised she doesn't climb right onto Robert's lap.

"You guys are sick," Natalie finally mutters, giving up

and turning away from them, clearly exasperated by this public display of stupidity.

"You're just jealous," Marissa says as she finally peels herself off Robert. "You've been acting like a total witch ever since you and lover boy Ben O'Conner broke up. Get over it, will ya, Nat? He certainly has."

By the time Natalie turns around to face them, her face white with rage, Marissa and Robert have gone back to kissing.

"You're such a tramp, Marissa," Natalie says, standing. "I'm surprised you don't just do it right here on the table." Then she picks up her half-full soda cup. "Maybe this will help cool you off." And she dumps it right over the two lunchroom lovers.

Okay, now I'm pretty sure we're going to have a catfight right here in the cafeteria. Marissa is so furious that she actually leaps at Natalie, who is looking a little scared as she moves back. Then Cesar and Jake grab Marissa, holding her at bay while Matthew and I whisk Natalie off to a safer location.

"How could you be so stupid?" I ask as we escort her from the cafeteria. "You know Marissa won't take—"

"I know Marissa is a tramp!" snaps Natalie. "And it's about time someone stood up to—"

"So did you want to get in a fight with her? Do you want to go back in there and roll around on the floor, clawing and scratching and pulling hair, while everyone gathers around to watch?"

Natalie doesn't respond to that, and I guess it makes

her think. I want to lecture her some more, but I suspect she'll be feeling bad enough before long. It seems like Nat really is her own worst enemy these days.

Later on, Cesar talks to me about the little fiasco. "I've really been praying for her, but it's like she's stuck. Do you think it's just that she can't get over Ben...or is it something else?"

Of course, I can't tell Cesar that it's because she lost her virginity and consequently thinks her life is over and is too embarrassed to take it all to God. Nat would kill me. "Yeah," I finally say. "She is kinda stuck."

"Is there anything we can do?"

"Besides praying?"

"Yeah, I mean, is there anything we can say to her?" He kind of laughs. "Well, besides me giving up my non-dating vow and asking her out. That might cheer her up."

"Or not," I say.

He nods soberly. "I guess that was a little vain on my part."

"No, that's not what I meant. For all I know she might still have that old crush on you. But I think her problems are deeper than that now."

"Oh."

"I guess I could try to talk to her again," I say halfheartedly. "I mean, it's been a while since I really had a heart-to-heart with her. And I know that she's still pushing God away. I could try to get her to rethink that."

Cesar looks encouraged. "That might be just what she needs, Kim. And isn't it ironic?"

"How's that?"

"Well, she used to be the one who was trying to spiritually encourage you. Now the table has turned."

"Yeah, the table just keeps turning, doesn't it?"

"I'll be praying for you guys," he assures me as we both head to class.

So on the way home, I tell Nat that I'm really concerned about her spiritual well-being. And what does she do? She just laughs. But her laugh is different now. It's very cynical and hard. Nothing like the Natalie I used to know.

"What spiritual well-being?" she finally says.

"Yeah, that's what I mean. It's like you've totally given up on God. And that just doesn't make sense. I mean, it's not His fault that you blew your vow, Natalie. But it's like you're blaming Him."

"I am not."

"Yes, you are." Then I try to bring it home by comparing her relationship with God to her friendship with me. I remind her that this thing with Ben has hurt me too. "And it's not like I had anything to do with it. But you've treated me pretty badly since it happened, Nat. How is that fair?"

Now she doesn't say anything.

"Because I want to be your friend," I continue. "And I need you for my friend. But ever since you and Ben, well, you know, it's like we're hardly even friends anymore."

"I was there for you when your mom died," she says defensively.

"Yeah, but that's about it. You were there that one night, and you were great. But that's where it ended. It's like you're not there anymore, Nat. Not for me and not for God. Even Cesar is worried about you. He thinks you're stuck."

"You told Cesar about—"

"No," I say quickly. "Of course not. I haven't told anyone. But everyone can see that you've changed. It's not like you're hiding it."

"Do you think they know?"

I consider this. "No, probably not. But I wouldn't be surprised if they start guessing. I mean, most people don't go through a total personality change just because someone breaks up with them. You know?"

"So maybe I should start acting like everything's fine?"

I sigh and shake my head. "I don't know, Nat. Wouldn't it be better if you got on your knees before God and made sure that everything is fine? Then it wouldn't just be a show. Don't you realize how much better you'd feel?"

Now she gets quiet again. And soon we're on our block.

"Maybe you need help, Nat," I finally say as I pull in front of her house. "Maybe you should see that counselor that your mom—"

"I'm not going to Marge!"

"How about Pastor Tony then?"

"Yeah, right. He's practically related to Ben."

"Related?" I'm trying to figure this out.

"Caitlin's aunt is married to Pastor Tony," she reminds me.

"Oh, yeah."

"Just forget about it, Kim." She grabs her bag and climbs out. "This is my problem, not yours." Then she slams the door.

"Right," I say as I drive away. "Like I don't get to share in your problem, Nat. Yeah, you bet."

Then I go in the house, and not for the first time, I desperately wish that the clock was turned back and Mom was puttering around in her kitchen. And I would sit down and tell her <u>everything</u>—even though I'd never really told her everything before. I would now. And while she might not have the answers, she would at least listen, and she would sympathize.

But the house was quiet as a tomb. Mom was not here. I'd call Matthew, but he's working on a mural at the library. Our art teacher, Mr. Fenton, set it up for him. Matthew is going to be able to use it as part of his portfolio.

"Does this mean you're still considering community college and then design school?" I asked him yesterday.

"I haven't decided," he admitted. "But I might as well keep my options open."

"How long until you have to decide?"

"Noon on Friday."

So I figure all I can do is be supportive of him and wait. I'm not even sure what I'd want him to do, I mean, if it were up to me. Which it's not, thank goodness. I suppose the selfish side of me would like to have him still living here and going to community college—at least for a year. But the academic side of me would be proud to have a boyfriend who's attending an Ivy League school. More than anything, I'd like to have Matthew surrender his life to God so that He could do the leading.

After walking around my silent house, I finally decided to practice my violin. Although I've memorized "Ave Maria" (the solo I'll be playing for Caitlin O'Conner's wedding in a couple of weeks), I know that it's good to practice it, to make sure that I've got it just right. Still, it's hard to play it sometimes…because it always makes me think of Mom. I first learned it so I could play it for her at Christmas.

And as I played this afternoon, I wondered what Mom was doing and if she could hear me playing. I wondered about heaven and tried to imagine what it would be like not to be living in an earthly body anymore. Finally, I couldn't focus on the notes because of the tears, and once again, I had to just put my violin away.

Then I remembered my mom's letter to me and how she told me to enjoy the sun and the birds and the flowers. So I went outside and walked around for a while. And I have to admit that it felt better out there. The sounds of birds, cars, lawn mowers—all of it was comforting to me. Still, how long will it take for this ache to go away? Or will it ever?

Then I heard the phone ringing inside and ran back in to get it. It was Natalie, and she was calling to tell me she was sorry. I asked her if this meant she was ready to get some kind of help, but she told me she didn't need any, and I just didn't know what to say to that. But I thanked her for apologizing, then told her unless she really wanted to talk, I had homework.

Of course, she didn't really want to talk—not really talk. So we hung up, and I went online to check my e-mail. I've had posts from Maya almost every day. And for the most part, they were gloomy and depressing. Her life is really sad. Aunt Shannon is either bouncing off the walls or practically in a coma. Maya plays the parent role, and how she manages to do any schoolwork (and it sounds like she doesn't do much) is a mystery.

I try my best to encourage her, but it feels like a lost cause. I think the best thing for Maya would be to go to school and just let Shannon take care of herself and clean up her own messes. But every time I say as much to Maya, she gets defensive. So then I think, maybe she likes her life just the way it is. But if that's true, why does she complain so much?

Now that I think about it, she reminds me of Natalie. Neither one of them are happy with their current status, and yet they don't do anything to change things. I don't get it. And so after I finish my homework, I answer some letters, and one of them is sort of along this line. The funny thing is, with my column, I can answer people's questions, and for all I know they actually take my advice.

Anyway, that's what I tell myself. And so I suppose my column is kind of like a comfort zone—like I have some control—although I'm pretty sure it's just a delusion.

Dear Jamie,

My grandma came to live with us last year because she "couldn't take care of herself anymore." At first I felt really sorry for her and helped out as much as I could. But now I'm onto her game. You see, she sits around all day, acting as if she can't do anything for herself. She has this walker and needs help to do everything—like getting dressed, bathing, eating, you name it. But I caught her once when she thought no one was home, and she was up and moving around and acting perfectly fine. But when she saw me, she acted like she was about to faint and collapsed in the nearest chair. I told my mom, but she thought I'd imagined it. I told my grandma that I wasn't going to "play along," and she can do things for herself. But what I want to know is, WHY DOES SHE DO THIS? Why does she want to live like an invalid when she's not?

Confused Granddaughter

Dear Confused,

I'm not sure why your grandma does this. But for some reason people get stuck in strange behaviors sometimes—and the reason they continue is because they think they are getting some kind of "payoff." For your grandma it might be attention. Or maybe it makes

*her feel loved to have your family caring for her. I
suggest you ask her why she's doing this. Of course,
she might not tell you, or she might continue to deny
that she's even doing it. In the meantime, hang in there.
And instead of being hard on her, why not use this as
an opportunity to get to know her better. You might be
surprised at what she has to offer. She might be
surprised too!*

   Just Jamie

I learned about that "payoff" thing on a "Dr. Phil"
show. And I have to say it made sense at the time. So
now I have to ask myself, what is Natalie's payoff in
keeping this wall up between her and God? Especially
considering how tight she used to be with God. What
can she possibly get from this kind of isolation and self-
punishment? I think and think about this, and finally I
come up with something. Okay, I could be totally wrong,
but it's all I've got at the moment.

   Pride. I hate to say it, but I think Natalie always had a
fair amount of pride when it came to being a Christian,
or what her megachurch was doing, or even in her own
beliefs and convictions. And I think it hurt her pride to
fail in this area, like she sees herself as this fallen,
unredeemable person now. As ridiculous as it seems—
when you consider how Jesus is the only One who can
remove our sins—I think it's her pride keeping her from
coming to God. Like if she stays away, she won't have to
admit that she's blown it.

Okay, that sounds really lame, and I'm probably just spinning my wheels, but it's the best I can come up with at the moment. Anyway, I might just ask her about it. Well, when the timing seems right. Which might not be ever.

Seven

Saturday, May 18

Matthew took me over to meet his grandparents tonight.
I was really looking forward to it and was all ready to be
impressed since I know that: 1) they are very wealthy,
and 2) they are very into really good education. And call
me shallow, but those two things definitely get my
attention.

It's not that I'm unimpressed with Matthew's mom. I
mean, she's a nice person and all, but she's so totally
different from me and my family. Maybe it's just her
artsy, creative ways, but she's kind of weird too. It's like
she enjoys getting noticed—whether it's for her strange
sense of style (she likes to wear clothing from other
countries) or the Bohemian way she decorates her home
or the theater crowd she hangs with. She's just very
different than what I'm used to.

So when we pulled up to the elder Barclay's house, make that <u>mansion</u>, I felt myself being instantly pulled in. You enter through a big metal gate, and their home is a stately white colonial-style house with big round columns and a circular driveway paved with bricks— kind of like a scene from "Gone with the Wind," but we don't live in the South. The grounds were immaculate with large trees, some that were blooming, growing in just the right places. Really beautiful.

"Wow," I said to Matthew as he parked his old pickup in front. "This is very nice."

Matthew nodded, seemingly unimpressed, but then why should he be since he's grown up around this? Still, it caught me by surprise since it's so totally different from how he and his mom live. As we walked up to the front door, I was glad that I hadn't worn jeans. It was such a nice sunny day that I'd opted for a skirt and top, actually one of the outfits Aunt Shannon had foisted upon me during her visit. But according to her, it was very chic. And after I tried it on again at home, I think I could almost see it.

Matthew didn't ring the doorbell but just walked right in. Naturally, I followed. But before we were halfway through the foyer (a room as big as our living room with marble floors and a staircase that swept in a wide circle like something out of a movie set), we were met by a maid.

"Matthew," she said with a smile. "Your grandparents are out on the terrace."

I suppressed a giggle—out on the terrace—I really was beginning to feel like I was in a movie and even wishing I had a script! We heard voices as we walked through a beautifully furnished room and toward the open doors that led to the terrace, and I realized that we weren't the only ones invited to dinner.

"Who else is here?" I asked Matthew, suddenly feeling even more nervous.

"Some friends of my grandparents," he said absently. "Someone he wanted me to meet."

"Oh."

"Don't worry," he said quietly. "That'll just make it that much easier for us to slip out early if we get bored."

Then we went outside and suddenly introductions were being made. The "friends" of his grandparents turned out to be the dean of Mr. Barclay's alma mater, as well as a law professor and the two distinguished men's wives. The group seemed to be enjoying a happy reunion, and I couldn't help but feel like an intruder, not to mention excess baggage. All attention seemed riveted onto Matthew, and to my surprise, he seemed to enjoy it. It was obvious that this was a well-planned mission to talk him into attending their prestigious school.

Occasionally, I'm sure out of politeness, a question would be directed to me such as: "What are your plans for college?" or "Do you have any extracurricular interests?" And while I did my best to answer in an intelligent fashion, I was under the distinct impression that they couldn't care less.

The funny thing about all this is that my GPA is higher than Matthew's, and my chances of getting a music scholarship for violin are probably better than Matthew's would be for art. Also, if I wanted to blow my own horn, I could tell everyone that I am the famous writer of a syndicated advice column. Instead, I was forced to say that I had recently been interested in journalism as a major.

Then Matthew mentioned that my dad was the managing editor of the local paper, and they all smiled indulgently, as if that was a "nice little occupation," although not nearly as impressive as their illustrious careers in law and education.

It turns out that Matthew's grandfather recently retired from "the bench." After a successful law career, Mr. Barclay became a high-level judge. If I'd been paying attention or been in trouble with the law, I should've been aware of that. I'm guessing my dad knows who he is. I suppose I should've asked. Oh, well.

As dinner wore on, I wondered why I felt so thoroughly disengaged. Almost as if I were on the outside just observing. Was it because Matthew was the center of attention and I was a little nobody? Which actually seemed odd since I don't usually like the limelight anyway. Or was it just that I felt like such an alien in their somewhat exclusive world of wealth and influence? And that didn't even quite fit, because I think in some ways I could fit better into that than Matthew.

Then it occurred to me that I was the only one in the

group of different ethnicity, and I got to thinking perhaps that was it. Or maybe it was because I was the only Christian in the group. Or at least I assumed that was the case, based on the consumption of alcohol and some of the language and off-color college stories I was hearing.

But the truly amazing thing about the whole evening was how Matthew seemed to be getting more and more pulled in. And finally when the dean really pressed the question to him, reminding Matthew that they'd already extended the deadline and this was absolutely his last chance, Matthew said that he'd made up his mind.

"I think my grandpa is right." He turned to Mr. Barclay. "I should go ahead and accept this generous offer."

Of course, this made the old guys very happy, and this naturally called for another round of drinks. "And bring out the champagne," Mr. Barclay called out. "We'll all make a toast."

I felt a little silly refusing their offer of champagne, but I knew it was right for me to do this. But Matthew accepted a glass, and I couldn't really blame him since it was his life they were toasting. I raised my water glass and echoed their well wishes, but all I wanted was to go home. And I have no idea why, but I really missed my mother right then. And I actually felt on the verge of tears, which seriously aggravated me. Why is that?

Finally, it was time to leave. I thanked Matthew's grandparents for inviting me. And they were more gracious than they'd been all evening, thanking me for

coming and thanking me for encouraging Matthew to
follow in his grandfather's footsteps.

"What did they mean by that?" I asked Matthew once
we were back in his truck.

"By what?"

"Thanking me for helping you to make this decision."

"Oh, I told them that you thought it was a good idea
for me to go there."

"I did?" I tried to remember exactly what I'd said. I
thought I tried to see the positive side of both options.
But perhaps I appeared to lean in this direction.

"Yeah, you said it was a great opportunity, Kim. Don't
you remember?"

"I guess so. And it is a great opportunity. If that's
what you want."

He didn't say anything.

"Is that what you want?"

He kind of shrugged. "Maybe I'm not entirely sure
what I want. I mean, it's not like I can predict the future.
But getting free tuition at such a prestigious college…well,
I guess I wonder how I can go wrong with it."

"And your art?"

"I can still pursue that."

"Will you?"

"Of course."

Still, I'm not so sure. When I got home, I went online
and did a little research on Matthew's "college of choice,"
and I wasn't all that surprised to see that they offered
very little in the way of art degrees. The only thing I

could find was "art and archaeology," and it sounded like
it had more to do with art history than anything else. But
I'm sure Matthew knows all this. Besides, he could
always change his mind after he spends a semester
there. And maybe free tuition is more important to him
that I realized.

Even so, I feel sorry for him. It's as if he got cornered
tonight, like all the big guns were pointing at him, and he
threw up his hands and said, "I surrender." Too bad he
can't do that when it comes to God. That's where he
really needs to surrender.

Finally, I just couldn't stand to think about Matthew
and his "future" anymore. So I decided to answer some
column letters. I think it's my little escape hatch
sometimes. My dad left a new batch in the familiar
manila folder on my desk. One letter in particular caught
my attention. It was a handwritten letter sealed in an
envelope with "To Just Jamie" on the front.

Apparently it was hand-delivered to the newspaper.
But something about it looked familiar, so I dug in my
box of old letters until I found one that looked just like it.
It was the letter that Charlie Snow (owner of the
newspaper) gave to my dad last fall. It was written by
his daughter Casey. And the small, neat handwriting
looked identical.

Casey's first letter had to do with God, and it came at
a time when I would have nothing to do with God, and
consequently I had a hard time answering her questions.
Of course, that has all changed, so now I'm thinking I

ought to be able to handle another Casey letter. Besides
that, she's also been on my prayer list since it seemed
she was really searching for spiritual answers.

Dear Jamie,
    I don't see why life has to be so hard. Sometimes I
just feel like giving up completely. How do people keep
going when it seems as if all they get is pain and
heartache and sadness? Sometimes the idea of dying
sounds like it could be a huge relief. Like just going to
sleep and never having to wake up again. What would
be wrong with that?
    Tired of Hurting

Wow, it sounds like Casey is having a really hard
time. And it makes me wonder what's going on in her
life that would get her to such a low place. I'll have to
ask Dad about this. In the meantime, I'll write a response
and make sure it goes in the next edition.

Dear Tired,
    You sound like you're really depressed. Depression
can have lots of causes—from things as simple as
messed-up relationships to eating the wrong foods. But
you need to talk to someone about this now—whether
it's your family doctor, a counselor, a pastor, or a
trusted and mature friend. You need to let someone
know that you're feeling this blue. And then you need to
get help (like counseling, therapy, medication…). When

*I feel discouraged, I find that it helps to pray, but
sometimes that's not enough. Don't be afraid to admit
that you have a problem—and to get help. We all go
through dark times, but the truth is, they don't last
forever. You need to make it to the other side so you
can see all the good things life has to offer. I'm praying
for you!*

    Just Jamie

I print out a copy of my response, along with Casey's
letter, for my dad to see. I suspect he's gone to bed,
since it's pretty late and the house was quiet when I got
home. But when I go into his den to leave the letters, I'm
surprised to see that he's in his chair. His head is leaned
back and his eyes are closed, and for one freaky second,
I think that he's dead! But then I hear him quietly
snoring, and I realize that he's only asleep.

I go over and gently nudge him. "Dad, don't you
want to go to bed to sleep?"

He jerks awake and looks at me with surprised eyes.
"Oh, Kim, you startled me."

"It's after eleven. I thought you were in bed."

"When did you get home?" he asks.

"About an hour ago."

"Did you have a nice time?"

"I guess so." I'm not sure how much detail to go into
since Dad really does look tired. He's got dark circles
under his eyes.

"What's that?" He glances at the papers in my hand.

So I sit down and quickly relay the contents of the letter and how I'm pretty sure it's from Casey Snow. Then he reads it for himself and just sadly shakes his head.

"She sounds so hopeless," I say.

"I wonder if Charlie knows..."

"Is there some way you could let him know, without giving it away...I mean, about the letter?"

"I'll see what I can do."

"Are you okay?" I ask him, worried about how tired he looks.

He removes his glasses and rubs the bridge of his nose. "I guess I'm as okay as I can be, Kim." Then he sighs. "It's not easy, you know."

"I know."

Then we both just sit there in silence.

"They have therapy groups," I finally say, "to help you to deal with grief and loss."

He nods. "But I'm just not a therapy group kind of guy."

"You can talk to me..."

He kind of smiles. "Thanks. And you can talk to me."

"But we don't..."

He scratches his head. "I guess I'm not even sure what to say, Kim. Just that I miss her. I miss her so much." And then his voice cracks, and he's starting to cry, and now I don't know what to do. So I stand up and go over and put my hand on his shoulder.

"Me too, Dad."

But he doesn't say anything else. He just keeps crying, and I feel like my heart is being broken into lots of pieces—it just hurts so much to see him hurting. And I want to tell him about how I suddenly missed Mom at dinner tonight, but then it doesn't seem important. Especially compared to what he's feeling. Finally, he reaches in his pocket for a handkerchief, wipes his eyes, and blows his nose. "I think I'm okay now," he mutters. "Thanks, Kim."

"I guess it just takes time," I say, knowing how lame that sounds.

He nods. "I'm sure you're right, honey."

Then we say good night. And while I'm sure that we must've comforted each other, at least a little, I feel more upset now than I did when I walked into his den. It's like my dad needs something, something deep and urgent and desperate, and I have no idea how to help him to get it. Maybe no one can. No one human, that is. And so I pray for my dad tonight. I pray that God will reach into those lonely places inside of him and make him well. And I believe that it can happen.

Eight

Sunday, May 26

Between Nat's never-ending moodiness, Matthew's growing conflict with his mother (after he informed her of his education decision), my dad's silent and unshakable grief, Maya's increasingly disturbing e-mails about her mom's addiction problems, and my own personal sadness—this has been a very long week indeed.

But I got dressed up and tried to shove all that behind me as I went to graduation last night. Matthew's mother had invited me to sit with her, and I was well aware that she did not intend to sit with the grand-parents. Fortunately, she got there in time to save us some fairly good seats, and it was easy to spot her from the floor since she was wearing this wild purple and gold outfit—I believe she said it came from Nepal.

Normally, I think graduations are pretty boring, but as I considered that this would be me (next year), I found I was paying closer attention to the details. Okay, call me narcissistic, but it's hard not to imagine what it'll be like, especially since I have a fairly good chance at valedictorian.

But realizing that I was being fairly self-absorbed, I turned my focus to Matthew, appreciating once again how tall and handsome he is (some people think he looks like Ashton Kutcher), and I guess I felt a little proud knowing that he was <u>my</u> boyfriend. Okay, now I really sound shallow. But he did look awfully good as he walked across the platform to get his diploma. And his mom and I clapped and cheered for him like groupies.

I was caught off guard seeing Chloe Miller getting her diploma too. I'd sort of forgotten that she was graduating early, since I still think of her as part of my class.

"I'll still relate to our class," she told me a week ago. "But this is just better for my music and my career. The opportunity was there, so I figured why not get it over with."

"And I'm sure it doesn't hurt that you're so smart," I teased her.

"You should talk," she tossed back. "You could've easily done the same."

And I know that I could've graduated a year early, if I'd wanted, but then I wouldn't have a chance at valedictorian. And for whatever reason, maybe because my mom was valedictorian of her senior class, this is still important to me. And I can almost imagine my mom watching me as I one day receive this honor, high up there from her front row seat in heaven. More than ever, I need to believe this.

"What do you think of Matthew's college choice?" his mom asked me in what I'm sure she hoped sounded like a somewhat nonchalant tone of voice, as if she wasn't as freaked over this recent turn of events as Matthew had been telling me. The grads were just starting to file out, with lively band music filling the gym as they happily paraded past. Thankfully, since it was getting hot in the gym, they were leaving much more quickly than they came.

"I was a little surprised," I admitted.

"You and me both." She used a tissue to blot perspiration from her forehead.

"I think he's really talented," I continued. "In art, I mean, well, and other things too. But I guess I thought he'd want to go to a school with a stronger art and design focus."

She nodded as we stood. "That's what I thought too."

We kicked the subject around a bit more as we slowly made our way down the steps, out of the crowded gym, and finally outside to where all the grads were in various stages of unzipping their gowns, tossing their hats, and generally making lots of we've-just-been-released-from-captivity kind of noises. We stood off to the sidelines, and I listened to her continuing to obsess over Matthew's life, his wasted talent, his disappointing college choice, his ill-planned future. But thankfully, as soon as he joined us, she discontinued her monologue, and we both offered our hearty congratulations.

But even as we were patting him on the back and commenting on how stuffy it was in the gym, his grandparents were pressing through the crowd to join us. Matthew, showing his usual good manners, included them in our little group, but his mother looked like she was about to explode. Wanting to avoid a bad scene, I asked her if she wanted me to get her some punch from the refreshment table.

"I'll come with you," she said in a tightly controlled voice.

And that's how it went. Matthew's mom acting as if his college choice and his grandparents' involvement were both a personal affront to her. And I just tried to remain supportively neutral, or stay out of it altogether. Finally, the stress was getting to me, so I told Matthew I was heading home so I could change my clothes for the all-night party.

"Pick you up around nine?" he said.

"Yeah." I waved and told the others good-bye.

Fortunately, the all-night party was much less stressful, and we ended up spending a lot of time hanging with Chloe and Cesar (who had come as her "date but not a date"—they made this very clear). Anyway, the four of us were really having a lot of fun, although I was ready to call it a night by 2 AM. However, with the lockdown in place, we were forced to stick around until seven when they started serving breakfast.

"Let's go to church," Chloe said after we finished breakfast. "We've got just enough time to make it to early service."

To my surprise, Matthew didn't protest. And the four of us went to church together in Chloe's VW van. It was actually pretty cool.

"Thanks for coming to the party with me," Matthew told me as he dropped me at home later that morning. "I probably wouldn't have gone if you hadn't."

"It was fun," I told him. "Exhausting, but fun."

"Yeah, I'll probably sleep all day now."

Then we kissed and said good-bye. But it was strange being dropped off at home after a date in the morning. I almost expected Dad to say something, although he knew what was going on, but he didn't appear to be home. I was hoping that meant he went to church. Although this would be a first for him since Mom died. Still, I've been praying for him to get back into it. Maybe that's where he is right now. Anyway, I know where I'm headed. My bed never looked so good!

Wednesday, May 29

I'm seriously worried about Nat. It's like she's trying to disappear off the face of the planet. I spoke to her last week, but I haven't actually seen her once this week. She hasn't wanted a ride to school. And I think she might've actually skipped some classes. Not that teachers are paying much attention since this is the last week of school, the seniors are gone, and everyone else is acting like summer vacation has already started.

But back to Nat. It's like she's going off the deep end. And while I know she's not my personal responsibility, she is my best friend. Yes, best friend. I've decided that even though she's not acting anything like a best friend, I still need to remain loyal to her, and I will continue to consider myself her best friend.

And I'm pretty sure she hasn't talked to anyone else about what's bugging her, specifically the Ben thing. According to her mom, who I even called at her workplace Monday since I was so concerned, Nat has not been to see a counselor and has no intention of doing so. Poor Mrs. McCabe has just about given up.

"I don't know what's wrong with her," she told me, clearly exasperated. "She's even been fighting with Krissy and Micah lately. And then she holes up in her room and refuses to talk to any of us. When I call her on it, she either blows up or threatens to run away. And I was so fed up last night that I told her to just go ahead. I know that was bad on my part, but I don't know what to do with her." She sighed loudly. "Oh, by the way, Kim, how are you and your dad doing these days?"

Of course, I acted as if things were okay, like Dad and I were just fine, moving on, getting over it. Yeah, right. But I just didn't have it in me to toss more crud on her ever-growing pile.

"I've been meaning to bring you guys a lasagna," she said. "I know it's kind of late, but life's been so crazy with Nat and all. Besides, I figured you'd be overwhelmed with food...at first..."

"That's so thoughtful of you, but don't worry about it. We're fine, really."

So then I tried to call Nat, but she was not picking up. I considered going over and barging in on her, but I didn't want to get her all mad at me. I figure it's better to stay on her good side, or else she might not have anyone to talk to. So I sent her an e-mail, just saying that I missed her and cared about what she was going through and wanted to talk.

Then this afternoon as I was going through letters for the column, I picked up this envelope that looked freaky familiar—it's exactly like this juvenile set of Hello Kitty stationery that I got Natalie when we were like twelve. Of course, I'm sure Nat has either used it up or thrown it away by now. But as I looked at the writing on the envelope (careful all-capped block letters that almost looked as if they'd been written to cover up the real handwriting of the sender), I was curious. I opened the envelope to find that the letter was computer printed.

Dear Jamie,

I think I am pregnant, and I can't talk to anyone about it. I have always thought that abortion was wrong, but now I am actually considering it, because I know that being pregnant will ruin my life. It's already ruining

my life. Sometimes I feel like I'm going crazy or that I
might kill myself. I want to know two things. Do you
think abortion is wrong? Do you think abortion is safe?
2 Scared 2 Talk

Oh, man! I have a really creepy feeling that Nat wrote
this letter. It would explain everything. It's so tempting to
call her right now, to ask her if she's pregnant, but that
would blow my cover. And then what? The next column
comes out in Friday's edition. If I make sure this letter
makes it, I can act like I read the letter in the paper, and
it made me wonder if she might possibly be worried
about something like that. I know it sounds hokey, but I
think it's my best plan. In the meantime, I am really
going to be praying for Nat. And I'm praying that God
will help me to answer this.

Dear 2 Scared,
    You definitely sound freaked. But I wonder why you
feel so scared about being pregnant. My guess is that it's
inconvenient and embarrassing. But stuff like that
happens to lots of people, and you just have to face up to
it and get over the initial shock. First of all, I suggest you
talk to someone—anyone—about what's going on. You
need a friend to lean on right now. As far as abortion
goes…I personally think that extinguishing an innocent
human life just to make yourself "feel better" is wrong. Is
it safe? According to my research, like any other invasive

*medical procedure, it has risks involved—but the greatest
risks are to the unborn baby. And oh yeah, I've heard
that lots of women suffer from guilt and can require
counseling for years afterward. My advice to you is to
talk to someone—a parent, pastor, counselor, friend. Now!
    Just Jamie*

My hands are actually shaking as I type my
response. I feel almost certain this letter is from Natalie. I
mean, she's been so different lately. She's moody and
depressed, and it's hard to believe it's all because of
Ben's breakup. I know it's crazy, but it seems highly
possible that she could've written this letter. Or even if
this is a coincidence, she could be in a position like this.

Although I can't believe that Nat would actually
consider abortion. She's always been totally opposed to
it. She's even gone to protest demonstrations, the kind
where they carry posters of photographs of unborn
babies.

But when I reread the line where the writer says she
might even kill herself, I feel more freaked than ever.
What if this is Natalie? And suddenly Friday seems so far
away, and I wonder if there's something I can do sooner.
So I walk down the street to her house, knock on the
door, and after what seems like ten minutes, Krissy
answers.

"Hi Kim," she says. She has smears of chocolate all
over her face.

"Is Nat here?"

Krissy nods. "But she doesn't want to be bugged. I think she's taking a nap."

"I won't bug her," I promise. Then I go upstairs, tiptoe to her room, and open the door. And Krissy is right; Nat is peacefully sleeping. Well, I suppose that's not such a bad thing—maybe I'm overreacting. Although I think I've heard that women get sleepy when they're pregnant. But maybe I'm just blowing this all out of proportion.

"Tell her I stopped by," I say to Krissy as I'm about to leave. Then I look around the messy house—TV blaring, clothes and papers and stuff everywhere. "Are you guys okay?"

Krissy just shrugs.

"Where's Micah?"

She shrugs again. "I think he's at baseball."

"Oh." Then without saying anything, I start picking up the clutter, the old newspapers and junk mail, food dishes, dirty socks. And Krissy, without saying anything, actually follows my lead.

We end up in the kitchen, which is really a mess, and Krissy tries to help, but mostly she just sits on a stool and watches me as I load and turn on the dishwasher, then start scrubbing the sticky countertops.

"Why are you cleaning our house?" she finally asks.

I look up at her. "I don't know…I just wanted to help."

"Are you sad about your mom, Kim?"

I rinse the dishrag in warm water, then turn and use it on her chocolate-smeared face, and she only resists a little. "Yeah. I'm sad about my mom."

She nods with wide eyes. "I would be really sad if my mom died."

"Don't worry, that's probably not going to happen until you're an old, old lady with gray hair and false teeth."

She smiles. "What's wrong with Natalie?"

I rinse the cloth again. "I don't know. Maybe she's sad too."

"About your mom?"

"I don't know…"

I finish up, then make Krissy promise not to tell anyone that I did this.

"But Mommy will think I did it."

I laugh. "Well, don't lie to her, but don't forget, you did help out some."

She hops off the stool. "And I could go clean my room too."

I give her a little hug. "That's a great idea."

Okay, I know my little good deed hasn't solved any of Nat's problems, but I do feel a tiny bit better as I head for my house. Still, I will be so glad when Friday comes, and we can get this thing cleared up.

I probably overreacted to that letter. Of course, I must be totally wrong. That stationery is just a silly fluke. Nat is not pregnant; she's just brokenhearted and depressed over Ben.

And now I can even imagine telling her about that letter (once it's in the paper) and how I got so freaked that it might be hers. Then she'll reassure me that it most definitely is <u>not</u> hers, and maybe we'll even have a good laugh over it. And that will be the perfect opportunity for me to remind her that life really could be worse. "Look, Nat, at least you're not pregnant!"

Nine

Friday, May 31

I've almost forgotten about the letter in my column as I grab a glass of orange juice and get ready to head out the door. It's the last day of school and all I can think is—<u>summer, here I come</u>. And man, do I need a break. I can almost imagine doing nothing but vegging for a week or two. And anyone who knows me would know that's a little out of character.

Then I notice today's newspaper by the door, and I pause to flip it open to the page where "Just Ask Jamie" appears. The letter is the second one down, and I skim over it, thinking that it doesn't even sound like Nat to me now. Not that I really know what Nat sounds like anymore, since we hardly ever talk. But as I set the paper aside, I'm telling myself that I imagined the whole thing. Nat definitely did not write that letter. I'm also telling myself that with summer vacation here, I'll have more time and energy to spend with Natalie, and maybe I can get her to go to counseling, maybe even at my church. I think things will be changing for that girl soon.

As I go outside, I see her heading for their old Toyota pickup. Her head is down, and she looks like she's got the planet riding on her shoulders. "Want a ride?" I yell down the street.

She glances my way with what appears to be a blank expression, like she doesn't even recognize me, which is ridiculous. So I walk over there. "Want a ride?" I say again, smiling. "We can celebrate the last day of school."

She still looks pretty blank. "Yeah, okay, I guess..." she mutters as she puts her keys back in her purse.

As we're riding to school, I attempt to make small talk about the warm weather and how great it is that summer vacation is finally here, how much I'm looking forward to just kicking back. Regular stuff. Stuff to fill up the empty airwaves that surround us. But as usual, she's not responding, not participating, not really there even. Finally, I'm parking my Jeep in the school parking lot, and I turn to her in desperation. "Natalie, this is really starting to bug me."

She gives me that blank look again. "What?"

"You. The way you're acting." Then I remember the column. "In fact, I was reading that "Just Ask Jamie" column this morning, and there was this letter that I almost thought—" I stopped to laugh and brush it off. "Never mind," I say quickly, knowing I am going too far.

"What?"

"It was nothing…"

"No, Kim, what was it?" Her voice sounds a little anxious, like I'm actually getting a reaction from her.

"Oh, there was this letter in there. Some girl was afraid she was pregnant and was thinking about getting an abortion, and I…" I stopped talking to study her expression now. But I was surprised to see that old proverbial deer-caught-in-the-headlights look, like she knew exactly what I was talking about.

"It wasn't from you, was it?" I manage to ask.

She takes in a breath as her hand flies up to her mouth.

"Natalie?" My voice actually cracks. "Did you write that letter? Are you…" I try to pull my words together. "Nat, are you pregnant?"

And now she bursts into tears. I don't know what to say, how to act. But I think I have my answer. And it makes me feel sick inside.

We both just sit there in silence, well, other than the sound of her quiet sobbing. But I really don't know what to do or what to say. Admittedly, I am stunned. Totally stunned. And yet a small part of me feels a sense of satisfaction to have finally reached the truth, like a detective who's finally found the missing clue. But another part, a much larger part, is very frustrated and, I hate to admit, angry. I'm thinking, <u>why did she do this</u>?

"It's going to be okay," I finally manage to say. "You'll get through this, Nat."

She looks up at me with reddened eyes. "How can you even say that?"

"You will. You're a strong person."

"I am not."

"Okay, fine, you're not. But God is strong. And if you let Him, He'll make you strong too." I glance at my watch. "And even though this is the last day and I'm sure no one much cares, I don't want to be late for class."

"I don't know if I can go to school now," she says in a small voice.

"Whatever," I toss back at her. I cannot deal with this.

"Kim?" she calls out the open window as I start to walk away from the Jeep.

"What?" I turn and look at her, exasperation written, I'm sure, all over my face.

"I need to talk."

And then it hits me. I told her, rather Jamie told her, to talk to <u>someone</u>—anyone. And now I'm just walking away? I'm supposed to be her best friend, and I'm just walking away and leaving her with all this crud heaped on her. What kind of person am I?

"Okay." I go back to the Jeep and stand by the passenger side and try to think of what I should do. "Just let me go inside and let the office know...so I'll be excused, you know?"

Nat looks at me like I'm crazy, and okay maybe I
am a little obsessive, but I like keeping a good
attendance record at school. Of course, the receptionist
doesn't seem the least bit concerned when I ask to be
excused. As I fill out the form, I tell her it's a personal
matter, and she says, "Fine, have a good summer,
Kim." Like no big deal. So I just leave. That's it. School's
out for summer.

We drive around for a while, but we're both being
quiet, and finally I think, why not save my gas and just go
home since neither of our parents are around anyway?
We end up at my house, sitting in my living room but still
saying nothing. Somehow I know it's up to me to get her
to talk, but I have no idea how to handle this. Suddenly
I'm thinking, where is Jamie when I need her?

"Are you certain you're pregnant?" I finally ask. Okay,
I guess I'm hoping she might just be imagining the
whole thing. Maybe her big guilt trip has made her
psychotic enough to believe that God has smitten her by
allowing her to be pregnant when she really isn't. Who
knows?

"I haven't done a test."

Okay, there's a small ray of hope. "Then it's possible
you might not be pregnant, like maybe you just think
you are."

"I missed my period in April and May."

"But you've always been irregular, Nat. And you've
been under a lot of stress lately. I've heard that stress
can mess with your cycle. Like women who are serving

in the armed forces in the battlefield, sometimes they just stop having periods altogether."

"Really?" she looks hopeful now. "Do you think...?"

"I think you need to do a test."

She sighs.

"Do you have one?"

"A home pregnancy test kit?"

"Yeah," I say it like "duh."

She shakes her head. "No, I cannot imagine going into a store and buying one, Kim. That's like saying I've done it for the whole world to see—I'd be so embarrassed."

"Look, Nat, if you are pregnant, the whole world is going to see anyway...eventually."

She doesn't respond.

"Let's go get one."

"A pregnancy test?"

"Yes, Nat. A pregnancy test. Come on, get up." I have to grab her hand and pull her from the couch. "You need to know for sure. I mean, what if you're not pregnant? What if you're putting yourself through all this worry and stress for nothing?" Fortunately, I have enough wits about me not to mention she's putting both of us through this worry and stress.

The Jeep is very quiet as I drive to the nearest Walgreens.

"I can't do this," she says as I park and turn off the engine.

"Can't do what?"

"I can't go in there and buy that thing, Kim. People will look at me. What if someone I know is in there?"

Well, this just makes me want to scream. "Fine," I practically shout. "I'll go get it." Then I slam the door and march inside.

Okay, once I'm in the section where the birth control goodies and whatnot are kept, I do start to feel uncomfortably conspicuous. I mean what if someone sees me here, sees me with an EPT kit in hand and a slightly guilty expression on my face? What would they think? What if I ran into a friend or co-worker of Dad's? What if it was Charlie Snow, owner of the paper and the only other person who knows that I write the teen advice column? What a great role model!

But I shove these thoughts aside as I pick up a box and walk to the back counter, the area where you pick up prescriptions, since it seems less busy and less visible back here. I put the kit, facedown, in front of the register and wait.

After what seems like more than five minutes, a man in a white pharmacist's jacket appears. "Can I help you?"

I point to the box. "Just that, please."

His brows lift, ever so slightly, but he turns it over and rings it up, and I'm somewhat surprised at how much the kit costs. I dig in my purse for the bills, avoiding his eyes as I do this, wishing that he would hurry and put that stupid box in a bag so I can get out of here ASAP. I push the cash toward him and wait as he counts it out, the box still sitting upright and visible—for the whole world, or at least the woman standing directly behind me, to see.

"You have to be very careful with this kind of home test," he says as he puts the bills into the register and removes my change. "Follow the directions precisely, or it might not give you accurate results."

"It's not for me," I say quickly, realizing he's probably heard this line before.

He finally counts out my change and slips the box into a white bag, concealing the personal nature of my purchase. Even so, as I walk through the store it feels like the bag is see-through, and I imagine that everyone knows, just by the shape and size, what's in that bag. And I feel totally humiliated.

Is this what Jesus meant when he said to "lay down your life for your friends"? Then it occurs to me that we could've ordered this item online and saved all this discomfort and embarrassment. But on second thought, that probably would've taken a few days to get here. And for some reason, time seems important right now.

"Here." I shove the package at Natalie. "You can thank me later."

She says nothing as I drive toward home. I am trying not to be mad as I consider how I could be at school right now, enjoying the last-day perks that they bring out as rewards for the kids who actually show up. They usually have goofy games and junk food, and it's more like a party than school. Instead, I feel like I'm being tortured. Why is life so hard? I decide to pray as I drive, asking God to make me a better person, a more understanding friend, and a less selfish human being. I hope He's up to the task.

Finally, we're back at my house. "You know where the bathroom is," I say. Then thinking I don't want her to botch this expensive, not to mention embarrassing-to-obtain, test, I add, "But let's read the instructions first." I do this aloud, but they seem pretty straightforward. "Got that?" I ask.

"Yeah." She takes the box from me and heads for my bathroom.

"Good luck," I call after her. Like what does that mean?

She comes out a few minutes later, but it does not look like good news.

"What?" I say with impatience. "Did the test work okay?"

"Apparently."

"What then? What are the results?"

"I'm pregnant." She flops back down on the couch and leans her head back.

"Really?"

"I knew it."

"You're really pregnant? You're certain?"

She nods without speaking. And I can see two trails of tears coming down her cheeks.

"It's going to be okay, Nat." I go over and sit next to her, putting a hand on her shoulder.

She just shakes her head. "No, Kim, it's not."

"I know it looks impossible right now, but God can help you through this. You have to let Him help you."

But no matter what I say, Natalie refuses to be encouraged. To her, this is the end of her life.

"What am I going to do?" she finally asks me, as if I should have all the answers.

"You're going to survive this, Nat. But you'll have to lean on God again. I'm certain that you will never make it on your own." Then it hits me. This isn't just Nat's problem. Ben, I assume it's Ben, has some responsibility here too. "And you'll have to tell Ben," I finally say.

"How do people do this?" she mutters. "How do you just walk up to someone, someone you once thought loved you, but now you know doesn't... How do you walk up to him and say, 'Hey Ben, you're going to be a daddy?'"

I shake my head. "I don't know. And come to think of it, maybe you shouldn't say anything just yet. I mean, until after Caitlin's wedding tomorrow."

Natalie almost laughs now. "That's right. Caitlin's wedding. Can you believe it? I was actually invited. Maybe I should go to the wedding and tell everyone that Caitlin's going to be an auntie. How do you think that would go over?"

"That would be cruel."

"I know. I'm not really going to do it." She starts crying again.

Now I put my arms around her. "Look, Nat, I know

you're hurting. And I know it's going to be hard. But I'm here for you, okay? And even more than that, God is here for you too. You've got to start leaning on Him again. He's just waiting for you to come and tell Him how much you need Him, that you're sorry…you know this stuff."

She pulls away. "I might know that stuff in my head, but I'm not ready to go there yet, Kim. Right now, I'm just very, very confused."

"Are you going to tell your mom?"

She looks shocked now. "Are you kidding?"

"How about a counselor? Maybe someone at my church."

"You mean Ben's church."

"It's God's church, Nat."

"Yeah, right."

"Well, you should probably at least see your doctor," I say. "I read that in the instructions for the pregnancy test."

"Sure, like I'm going to go to the family doc and tell him I'm knocked up. You bet."

"They have a confidentiality policy, Nat."

"For minors?"

I shrug. "How far along do you think you are?"

"Based on my calculations and what little research I've done, the baby would be due around New Year's. I'm about two months pregnant."

I slowly shake my head, like it's still sinking in. "This is so weird, Nat. I mean, I can't imagine you with a baby."

"No one said I have to have this baby, Kim. I haven't made up my mind yet."

"What do you mean?"

"I mean…I can get an abortion."

"But you're opposed to abortion, Nat. I've heard you going on and on about it, almost ever since I've known you. You and your mom even picketed the clinics. And you've got that Right to Life poster in your room."

"I took it down."

"But still…"

"People change, Kim."

"But an abortion?" I study my friend carefully.

"You used to act like you supported abortion, Kim."

I consider this. "I think I just liked to take the opposite position of you, playing devil's advocate, you know? And besides, that's before I became a Christian. And like you said, people can change."

"So we've flip-flopped. You're the conservative Christian now, and I'm the liberal—" She stops herself short of saying she's not a Christian. That gives me hope.

"I think you're just scared. I don't think you've really changed your position on anything. You're just feeling cornered, and you don't know what to do."

"Well, what would you do, Kim? I mean, if you were in my shoes?"

I want to tell her that, first of all, I wouldn't be in her shoes, but that sounds so mean and proud. And I remember how I used to feel when she came across sounding like that to me. "I'm not sure. But the honest truth is, I don't think I'd consider abortion."

"And why not?"

"Several reasons… For one thing, I think about my own birth mother. I'm sure she could've gotten an abortion, maybe she even considered it. But if she had…well…I wouldn't be here, would I? And then I think about Mom, and even though she's not around, I think she'd want me to have the baby."

"And then what?" she asks. "Drop out of school to change diapers?"

"I don't know, Nat. Maybe I'd consider adoption. I'm not sure. But why are we putting me on the spot? You're the one who's pregnant. You're the one who has to figure this out."

Our conversation is finally running out of steam. It is past noon and we both decide we are hungry. Eager to put this hot topic to rest, I offer to treat us to burgers and fries. "But let's not talk about pregnancy, abortions, or babies," I say as we drive to Dairy Queen. And once we get there, we just act like a couple of normal girls who are just starting summer break. And I have to say that Natalie is more like her old self. And it isn't too bad.

Okay, it was obvious she needed to talk to someone about this. It's like she had this pressure valve that needed to be released, and afterward she was actually able to relax a little. Even her face looked less stressed.

Of course, I realize this is just the beginning, and she'll need to talk again. And again and again. And she needs to come to grips with this whole thing. And hopefully, she'll reach the place where she can talk to someone else—someone with knowledge and experience—someone with better advice than I can give. Sure, I might sound good on paper as Just Jamie, but I don't think I'm cut out to advise Natalie. The truth is, I am feeling more stressed than ever right now. It's a heavy load to carry—being the only one (besides God) who knows that her best friend is pregnant. Like I needed this right now.

Ten

Saturday, June 1

As if playing a violin solo for a wedding isn't stressful enough—especially a wedding for someone as sweet and good as Caitlin O'Conner where you really don't want to mess up—I had to bear the additional stress of knowing that Caitlin's only brother, Benjamin, is the father of my best friend's unborn baby. I felt like I was playing a part in a soap opera! I tried not to think about that prior to the ceremony and certainly not as I played "Ave Maria."

In fact, as I stood there playing my solo, positioned off to one side in the front of the beautiful church with the stained-glass windows illuminated by the sun, the notes reverberating through the spacious sanctuary, I felt as if my mom was right there with me. It was one of those amazing moments when everything in life seems to be nearly perfect, like the universe is in order and God is smiling down on us. And even though I knew in my head that my mom was gone, I felt her presence with me in the strongest way—like I could almost reach out and touch her. And for those few brief moments, it was truly comforting.

And the wedding ceremony was beautiful. Not unlike the sort of wedding I've dreamed of having some day. But as I sat there watching the whole thing, it occurred to me that my mother wouldn't be there to help me with it, to plan all those details and to pick things out. And despite that earlier feeling of her presence, I began to miss her all over again. Fortunately a lot of people cry at weddings, and I doubt that anyone thought it strange that I had the sniffles too. And at least I was sitting off to the side in the shadows, where I doubt anyone noticed.

Afterward, I was tempted to skip the reception, except that I had already invited Matthew to be my date. Besides, it was supposed to be a very fun evening. And Chloe and Allie would be there, as well as others from the youth group. And of course, Ben. I would have to make sure to avoid any conversations with him. How awkward.

Natalie had come over to my house earlier this afternoon. She said it was to help me with my hair (for the wedding), but I think it was only to make sure that I was perfectly clear about Ben.

"You are not to say one word to him," she told me in a firm voice.

"Not even hello?"

She poked my head with the end of the comb. "You know what I mean, Kim. Don't say or do anything that could give this away."

"Do you really think I'd want to?"

"Well, you might do it accidentally."

"I'm not stupid, Natalie."

Finally, she was convinced. And my hair didn't look too bad either. "Thanks," I told her. "What do I owe you?"

She moaned and flopped down on my bed. "I feel like Cinderella."

"Huh?"

"You know, left out of everything. I didn't get to go to the prom. And now, even though I'm invited, I don't get to go to Caitlin's wedding."

"Why don't you go?"

She rolled her eyes. "Yeah, right. Caitlin invited me before Ben and I broke up. I'm sure she wants me to show up now."

"She probably wouldn't mind..."

"Well, Ben would. Besides, I might fall apart and tell everyone that I'm pregnant. No, it's better that I stay home. Just like Cinderella."

"What does that make me?" I asked. "The wicked stepsister?"

"No. But it just doesn't seem fair. I'm the one who should be Ben's date today. Especially considering...well, you know."

I just sadly shook my head. "You're right, Nat, it doesn't seem fair."

And the more I think about it, it really doesn't seem fair. I mean, Ben is just as much to blame for Natalie's situation as she is. And yet, he's out there doing things and having fun, and Nat's the one who's suffering. Even at the wedding reception tonight, Ben was with Torrey, laughing and dancing and whooping it up and having a great time. Meanwhile, poor Nat's stuck at home with morning sickness or whatever you call it. She told me that she's thrown up several times already. It must be miserable.

"Didn't you take any precautions?" I had asked her earlier this afternoon.

She kind of laughed. "Precautions?"

"You know," I continued. "Birth control. They teach about it in health class?"

"Think about it, Kim," she said with some impatience. "Ben and I were both Christians, both dedicated to abstinence. It's not like he had a bunch of condoms in his pocket. And I wasn't exactly on the pill, if you know what I mean."

"So you did IT without any protection?"

She sighed. "Yeah, at least the first time or two. I mean, it's not like we planned it all out."

"Obviously."

"We did use some things, you know, after that..."

I was tempted to ask her how many times they actually had sex, but it felt like "too much information," and so I didn't push her. But based on what she'd told me before, I didn't think they'd really done it too many times. Still, they'd done it enough to get pregnant—or to transmit an STD, although that would've been unlikely since they'd both been virgins.

One of the uncomfortable things about Natalie's pregnancy is that I have to keep it to myself. She made me promise not to tell anyone, including (and specifically) Matthew. And it's hard to act as if everything's fine when I'm feeling pretty freaked for my best friend.

Like tonight at the wedding reception. I suppose I was being a little quiet as we sat at a table off to one side. And in all fairness, that was partly due to feeling sad about Mom, but I was also feeling seriously irked as I watched Ben and Torrey clowning around as if they didn't have a care in the world.

"What's wrong?" Matthew asked me.

"Nothing," I said quickly.

"Come on, Kim. I know when something's bugging you. What's up?"

I just shrugged and told him I was fine and not to worry. But he persisted. I suspect he thought it had something to do with him or us. Finally, I just told him about how it had occurred to me that Mom wouldn't be around to help with my wedding.

"I mean, if I ever have a wedding," I threw in. "It's not like I'm planning one." Then I laughed.

He didn't say anything, but he did seem relieved.

And it wasn't as if I'd lied to him exactly. It was true that I had been missing my mom. Still, it wasn't completly honest either. I'll be so glad when Natalie is ready to have this out in the open. Not that she'll send out announcements to everyone, but all this secrecy is stressing me out. Speaking of getting things out in the open, I answered a funny letter this week.

Dear Jamie,

I'm supposed to be pet sitting my friend's canary Tweety while she's at camp this week. After feeding Tweety yesterday, I accidentally left the cage door open, and he somehow escaped. By the time I figured it out, all that was left of him was yellow feathers, and my cat was nowhere to be seen. This is my question—do you think it would be wrong to replace Tweety with another canary that looks just like him? They have some great look-alikes at Petco, and I don't think my friend would be able to tell the difference. What would you do?

Bird Killer

P.S. Can you answer this privately since my friend reads your column?

So I sent Bird Killer a letter on Wednesday. Hopefully she got it in time.

Dear BK,

My experience is that honesty really is the best policy. It may appear simpler to lie (at first), but it can

*get really involved on down the line. For instance, what
if a mutual friend saw you buying a canary at the pet
store and informed your friend? Then what would you
do? I suggest that you break the sad news to her gently.
Tell her how very sorry you are and then offer to
replace Tweety with another bird and see what she
says. For all you know, she may be tired of birds and
want a guinea pig. Anyway, good luck.*

    Just Jamie

Too bad all of life's questions aren't that simple.

Sunday, June 2

Dad was acting really strange this afternoon. Not strange
as in stuck in his grief like he usually is, but today he
was really agitated and upset. He kept pacing around
and slamming cupboard doors and muttering and
complaining about everything...until finally I just had to
ask him if something was wrong.

At this point, he stops pacing and just looks at me
with this really odd expression. "I was about to ask you
the same thing."

"Huh?" Okay, now I'm more confused. I mean, he's
the one who was slamming doors and pacing and stuff.
"What do you mean?"

"Is something wrong with you, Kim?"

"No. Well, nothing other than the regular stressful
stuff of life, that is."

"What kind of stress?"

His sudden interest in my life makes me curious. I'm not sure if he's trying to be a good dad or to make up for being so distant lately or what exactly. But I decide to play along. "As you know, I still struggle with missing Mom a lot. Like yesterday at the wedding. Well, at one point everything seemed so cool because it felt like she was right there with me, like I could almost feel her, you know? And then within minutes, I was crying because I knew she was gone and—"

"So you're having mood swings?"

I consider this. "Yeah, I guess so. I mean, it felt like she was with me and that was great, but then I realized she wouldn't be here for my wedding, to help me plan it and then—"

"Are you planning on getting married anytime soon?"

I frown at him. "No, Dad. But that's not the point. It's just that I would miss her being around to—"

"I miss her too, Kim." His tone is growing slightly impatient now. "But is there anything else that's bothering you?"

"Well, I've been kind of stressed over Natalie lately. She's been so depressed the past couple of months, and I'm not sure how to help her." I realize I can't go any further with that problem, so I change the subject. "And then there's Matthew…"

"What about Matthew?" Now Dad looks very interested, and I wonder if this isn't what's been getting at him all along.

So I launch into the whole story of Matthew's grandparents, the Ivy League school, how his mom is so furious at him for caving, how they've been arguing a lot, and how I'm not very happy with his choice either. And I'm not even finished explaining the whole thing when Dad cuts me off.

"So you're upset because Matthew will be going away to school? Leaving you behind, so to speak?"

"No, not exactly. Of course, I'll miss him and everything, but I guess I'm more upset that he's not following his dream."

"His dream?"

"Art. He loves art and design, Dad, and he's very gifted too. I was hoping he'd go to a really good design school that would help him to—"

"And that's all that's bugging you?"

Now I'm feeling pretty exasperated. "Isn't that enough? How much stress do you think I need anyway?"

"Well, I..."

And then I remember something else. "Oh, yeah, there's another thing, but you might not want to hear about—"

"No, Kim. Go ahead, I'm your Dad. I want to hear about everything."

"The truth is, I've been pretty worried about you too. I mean, you're not exactly yourself these days. I understand that it's hard for you, losing Mom, but I lost her too, you know. And you've been so closed up, and I know you're sad and hurting. But it's upsetting to know that there's nothing I can do about it, no way I can help you." I hold up my hands in pure frustration. "There, is that enough stress for you?"

He nods slowly. "That's a lot of stress, Kim. In fact, it's enough stress to make someone do something that's out of character. It might cause a person to make choices she might've otherwise reconsidered."

"What are you saying, Dad?"

"I'm just saying it's possible that all this stress has put you in a tough spot. And you may be dealing with something that's overwhelming to you, something you don't feel comfortable discussing with, well, me. And I realize that your mom's not here, and maybe you would've been more comfortable talking to her about some things. But Kim, I'm all you have right now. Is there anything you'd like to tell me?"

Okay, I'm looking at my dad like he's got three heads. I mean, what on earth is he trying to say? And why does he seem like such a complete stranger, not to mention a total doofus?

"I have absolutely no idea what you're getting at, Dad," I finally tell him. "But if you have something to say, could you just get it out into the open? You're really starting to freak me."

"The home pregnancy test," he mutters.

I feel myself jerking to attention now, as if I'm somehow guilty of something—other than being a good friend. Crud, why didn't I remember to throw it out in

the trash can outside? I know how Dad goes around
emptying wastebaskets on Saturdays. He obviously saw
it and jumped to conclusions. Why are parents so
obtuse?

"Oh, that."

"Yes, that." He studies me closely, as if he really
believes I'm the one who used it. And while I can
understand this mistake, it really irks me too.

"Well, it wasn't mine."

He looks unconvinced. "Really?"

"Really, Dad! That's perfectly ridiculous. I cannot
believe you would think that I am or that I would or that
I could—" I stop blabbering and just shake my head in
complete disgust.

"Kim, it looked like the test had been used..."

"Of course, it had been used. That's what it was for.
But I was not the one who used it."

"I see..."

"Dad!"

"Come on, honey. You can tell me what's going on.
I'm your dad. I love you."

The problem is I can NOT tell him. Not yet anyway. I
promised Natalie I wouldn't tell a soul.

"So what was the result of the test?"

Now I'm just plain mad. "It was positive, Dad. Are
you happy now? Positive in meaning that a baby is due
sometime around New Year's. Is that what you wanted
to know?"

But then I see his expression, and I know that I've

totally crushed him. He looks like he's about to have a heart attack or stroke or maybe just break down in tears. Why am I so cruel?

"I'm so sorry, Dad," I say quickly. "Let me explain." I pull out a kitchen stool for him. "Just sit down and take a deep breath. I'll tell you what's up."

He still looks worried, but at least he sits down and appears to be breathing.

"Look," I tell him in a calm voice, "this is the truth. The test really wasn't for me. And the person who used the test swore me to secrecy. I can't tell you who it is. But…" I consider another option. "I'll bet you could guess."

Suddenly he looks hopeful. "It's really not you, Kimmy?"

I firmly shake my head. "No way, Dad. It is most definitely not me. I promise you."

Relief washes across his face. And I can tell he's wondering who really used that test. "Well, I know it can't possibly be Natalie. That girl is so firm in her convictions, and I've even heard her talking about it numerous times. And as a dad, I must admit it is reassuring to hear. Your mother was always very impressed with that too."

"Right…" I try to keep my expression blank.

Dad looks slightly perplexed, and I know he can't begin to guess who used the kit. "Maybe it's not important that I know who it was, Kim. As long as I know it's not you."

"That's fine with me."

"And while we're having this little talk, I need to tell you how sorry I am for having been so detached lately." He shakes his head. "I just don't quite know how to function yet. Every little thing seems so difficult. I feel like I'm climbing a mountain sometimes, but the top is nowhere in sight."

"I know it takes time to get over this, Dad."

He kind of smiles. "Well, that surprise in your wastebasket really threw me for a loop last night. Maybe it's a bit like electroshock therapy, because I actually feel better now. I cannot begin to tell you how relieved I am that you're not the one who used that test. I'm not sure what I would've done if you had actually been pregnant. A man can only take so much."

"You and me both." Then I laugh. "But I do feel sorry for the girl who did take it. She's really devastated."

"Her parents probably are too."

Or they will be, I'm thinking. At least her mom. That is, if Natalie ever tells her—not that she has a choice exactly. Still, it won't be easy.

Eleven

Monday, June 3

It's about nine o'clock in the morning when I wake up to the sound of the phone ringing. I consider letting it go to the machine. This is my official first day of summer vacation, and I really had planned to sleep in. But thinking it could be Matthew, since he told me he'd call today, I decide to go for it.

"Kim?" says a vaguely familiar woman's voice.

"Who is this?"

"It's Grandma, dear. Is your father there?" She sounds urgent and slightly breathless.

"No. He's at work. Is something wrong, Grandma?"

"Well, I, uh, I don't know for sure…"

"What do you mean?" Now, I don't know my grandma all that well, other than she's dad's mother and she lives in Florida and is what Dad calls "eccentric" and what my mom used to call a "real character." Consequently her dramatic vagueness doesn't seem all that strange.

"Your Uncle Garth said your father called yesterday. I was out playing bingo, having a rather good game if I do say so. But Garth seemed concerned. He said the phone call was important, some kind of an emergency, I believe."

"Emergency?"

"Yes. But then you probably know how Garth can be. Sometimes he runs off like a chicken with his head cut off, so he might not have gotten his facts straight."

I can almost imagine this since I've heard that my Uncle Garth is somewhat eccentric too. "Yes, I suppose that's possible."

"Say, did you get my card, Kim?"

I force my sleepy mind to think and finally remember the card she sent right after Mom died. I know it was meant to be a sympathy card, but it was actually a get-well card. Although I suppose they work pretty much the same. "Yes," I tell her. "Thank you very much."

"We would've come for the funeral, but like I said in the card, I was having foot surgery that very same day. And my toes have been giving me such trouble. I just couldn't put it off. I know that Patricia would understand. Besides that, there's Garth, and well, he doesn't like to travel by plane much. But believe you me, you and Allen were both in our thoughts and our prayers. You must know that, I'm sure."

"Yes, I know, Grandma." But now I don't know what

to say. I'm not even sure why she called. "Uh, maybe you should try calling Dad at work." Then I give her the number.

"Garth thinks you ought to come out here to visit us," Grandma tells me before she hangs up. "He thinks you'd enjoy the gators."

"Alligators?"

"Oh, yes. We have dozens of them, coming right onto our property. They're as friendly as can be."

"Friendly?"

"Goodness, yes. Sometimes I throw kitchen scraps out to them, and they just gobble them up. Leftover fried chicken is the best. Why, I've even named a few."

"Fried chickens?"

She laughs. "No, darling, the gators. I've got Gloria and Bill Gator, named after the famous gospel singers. And then there's Mr. Farley; I named him after the postman."

"I hope you're careful, Grandma. I've heard alligators can be quite a problem." I don't mention that I've also heard that it's illegal to feed them in some areas, since I suspect she probably knows this.

"Oh, I respect them and they respect me."

"That's good."

"But I do think Garth is right."

"About?"

"About you coming out here to visit us, Kim. You haven't been out here since you were a wee little thing, and I'll bet you don't even remember that."

"I remember some," I tell her.

"Well, it's high time you came again."

I kind of laugh now. "Okay, Grandma, I'll think about that." Then we say good-bye. and I wonder why on earth I'd ever want to go out to Florida where my grandmother feeds kitchen scraps to the local alligators in her own backyard. I can just imagine her in her bright-colored muumuu and bedroom slippers. Good grief!

I'm barely out of the shower when the phone rings again. Running to get it, thinking this must be Matthew this time, I am surprised to hear Nat's voice on the other end. I'm usually the one who calls her these days.

"I've made a decision," she tells me in a flat-sounding but determined voice.

"Yeah?" I'm not sure what exactly she's referring to, but I'm guessing she wants to tell Ben, or maybe her mom, about what's going on with her. And if you ask me, it's about time.

"And I need your help, Kim."

"Okay," I tell her. "What's up?"

"I can't do this alone." Now her voice cracks slightly, and I think she's starting to cry.

"I'm here for you, Nat. Just tell me what you need me to do. I want to help you through this."

She sniffs and then continues. "Can you give me a ride today?"

"Sure," I say, knowing this means I'll have to cancel on Matthew. "Just tell me when and where."

"We need to leave here by one. I'll fill you in on the rest of the details later, okay?"

"Okay. I'll be ready at one."

Now I'm curious as to where we're going. Is she going to make an appearance at Ben's house? What if his parents are there? Or maybe she has it all figured out so they'll be at work. And as uncomfortable as it sounds, I guess this is the sort of news that should be communicated in person—face-to-face. Poor Nat. I pray for her to be brave as I get dressed.

I do a few chores around the house, and when Matthew doesn't call me by noon, I call him and leave a message saying that I won't be able to do anything with him until later, if at all. Not that he seems to care much, since he hasn't bothered to call me yet.

Finally, Nat and I are driving down our street, and I ask her where it is we're going.

"Downtown," she tells me with a wooden expression.

Now this throws me, and I wonder if this means she's going to tell her mom first. But I don't question this. I can tell she's having a hard time already. She doesn't need me to make it any worse.

When we are downtown, I start to turn in the direction of where her mom works, but Nat tells me to take a right instead. Without questioning this, I obey.

"Just three more blocks," she says. "On the left side."

As we get closer, I realize where it is we're going.

"Nat?" I say in a slightly high-pitched voice. "Are we going to Haven?"

Now everyone knows that (despite their slick ads about women's health, birth control, and whatnot) Haven Women's Clinic deals mainly in abortions—I've heard that they perform them right up into the third trimester. In fact, I wouldn't be the least bit surprised if Natalie's church has protested here in the past.

"They do pregnancy tests," she says, almost as if she's rehearsed this line.

"But you already know you're pregnant."

"Yes, but remember you said I should have a checkup."

"With your family doctor."

"Well, I can't take that risk. My mom might find out."

"But you're okay taking the risk of being seen walking into this place?"

She doesn't answer. And I have to ask myself, am I okay being seen walking into this place? Despite the vacant parking spots on the street, I notice a sign for "additional parking" and decide to park in back.

"Natalie," I try again as I turn off the engine. "Are you sure you know what you're doing?"

"I'm having a checkup." She climbs out and slams the door. "Just chill, Kim. This is hard enough without you making it any worse."

And so I keep my mouth shut, but I'm glad to be wearing my dark glasses as we walk through the back parking lot and enter through a back door that I suspect has been situated there just for people like us. I cannot believe that Natalie really wanted to come here. And I cannot imagine what her mom or people at her church would think if they knew.

She goes up to the reception area and tells them she has an appointment. They give her some forms to fill out, and we both go and sit in the waiting area. Okay, now here is the embarrassing truth—I don't want to be sitting in this chair. I don't want to touch anything. I don't want to be here at all. This place feels horribly evil to me. It's wrong. Totally wrong.

I glance over at Natalie, but she's completely composed, focused on filling out the form. And I know I better just keep my mouth shut. This is her life, not mine. But man, do I want to scream! So much so that my throat is actually starting to ache.

Finally, she finishes the form and returns it the receptionist. She comes back and sits down, crossing her legs and arms, almost as if to protect herself.

"Natalie?" I say quietly, almost a whisper. "You don't have to keep this appointment, you know. We could just leave, slip out of here, and you could go to another doctor, a regular doctor, maybe even my doctor, and—"

"I don't have money for that," she snaps.

"Maybe I could help you—"

"No." She turns and looks at me with angry eyes. "I told you I really need your help today, Kim. And what you're doing right now is NOT helping. Do you get that?"

"But, Nat—"

"Kim!"

I glance around, curious as to whether we're drawing attention since our voices have gotten louder, but the other people, mostly women and a few children, seem absorbed in their own lives and problems. We don't matter to them at all.

"Natalie McCabe?" calls a woman.

Nat looks over to the door and nods, then slowly stands, looking back at me with wide blue eyes.

"Do you want me to come in with you?" I ask meekly.

She just shakes her head. "No, I'll be okay."

"But, Nat—"

Then she walks away, goes through the door, and I'm left here to wonder, to speculate, to imagine. Okay, is this really just a "checkup" appointment like she said, or is it possible she's actually going in there to get an abortion? I've heard that women just walk into this place, have the procedure, and then walk out like it's no big deal. Is it possible that Nat is doing that today?

But how can that be? She's not even an adult. You can't get your ears pierced or a tattoo without parental consent. You can't even get an aspirin from the school nurse without a note from home or the doctor. How could it be that Nat might be having a dangerous surgical procedure, one that some people consider murder, and I'm the only one who knows about it? The mere idea is so freaky that I'm starting to feel sick to my stomach.

Finally, I am so antsy and worried I can no longer sit

still. I get up and start pacing. I read all the notices on the
bulletin boards. I pick up a dog-eared parenting
magazine and absently thumb through it. I consider
using the restroom just to waste time, but the idea of
touching anything in there, or here for that matter, is
really getting to me. It's like I can feel a great big case of
obsessive-compulsive disorder coming on. God, help
me!

I feel like I can't breathe. It's like I have to get outside
or I'm going to suffocate. I start to head for the front
door but then remember that the street is out there,
someone might see me, so I hurry to the back door
instead. When I get out to the parking lot, I practically
gasp to catch my breath.

"Looks like you need a cigarette break too," says a
woman who's sitting on a bench by the back door as
she lights up a cigarette.

"No," I tell her, moving away. "Just some fresh air."

I go over to the Jeep, unlock the door, and then just
stand there. It's not like I can get in and leave. I lean over
slightly, forcing myself to take some big deep breaths.
And I tell myself that I'm acting totally stupid. Natalie is
not getting an abortion. She is just getting checked.
Lighten up, Kim!

But I can still feel my heart racing, and I know I'm on
the verge of tears. The idea of Nat in there, doing God only
knows what—well, it's just too much. It makes me feel sick
and hopeless and really, really sad. And more than
anything else, I really want my mom right now! I want to

run to her and tell her what Natalie's doing and how it's upsetting me and how I just can't take this anymore. I want her to put her arms around me, stroke my hair, and say, "Kimmy, it's going to be okay. Everything's going to be okay." But she can't do that anymore.

Finally I get inside the Jeep, and leaning my head against the steering wheel, I try to pray. But it's like the words are stuck inside of me. I try and try to pray—but I can't. And finally I just break down and cry. For a long time.

When I stop crying and look at my watch, I'm shocked to see it's nearly three o'clock. I lock up my Jeep and hurry back inside, worried that Natalie's appointment is over and that she thinks I've abandoned her, so she's gone off and called a taxi. And when I get back inside, I don't see her anywhere. So I go to the receptionist.

"I'm here with my friend, but I had to go out for a while. Can you tell me if she's finished her appointment yet?" Then I give her Nat's name.

Thanks to some kind of privacy policy, the woman refuses to tell me anything regarding Natalie. So I go back and sit down. Surely, Nat would've checked the parking lot before trying to leave without me.

About fifteen minutes later, Natalie comes out. I hurry over to her, worried that she might be upset—especially if she's just gone through an abortion, which is my greatest fear.

"Are you okay?"

She just shrugs. "Let's go."

When we're in the Jeep, I ask her again. "Is everything okay, Nat? That seemed like a pretty long checkup."

"They have lots of questions and stuff," she says without looking at me. "And plus they were busy."

"So, did they do a pregnancy test?"

She nods. "It was positive. Big surprise."

"And so?"

"So what?"

"So, is that it? You know you're pregnant for sure...and now what?"

"I have an appointment for next week."

"An appointment?" I'm trying very hard to remain calm. I've already had my little breakdown. Nat doesn't need to see me falling apart.

"You know," she says. "To get rid of it."

"Get rid of it?" My voice sounds like a five-year-old.

"Yes, Kim. I've decided it's my only option. I will get rid of it. And no one will ever have to know. It's really the best way to go."

No one will ever have to know? What about me? But I don't say anything. I just try to get us safely home. By the time I pull in front of Natalie's house, I am feeling numb. I don't just mean emotionally numb, although that would make sense, but my fingers are tingling, and I'm worried that something might actually be physically wrong with me.

"Thanks," she says as she opens the door. "Sorry I

had to drag you through this with me."

I force a very pathetic smile. "It's okay, Nat. I said I was here for you."

"And next week?" She looks at me hopefully.

Everything in me wants to scream and shout, NO! No way! Never! Forget it! But she looks so hopeful—more hopeful than she's seemed in months. So I simply nod and say, "Yeah, I guess so."

Of course, by the time I get in my house I am asking myself, why on earth did I agree to go with Natalie next week? Am I freaking nuts?

Feeling the need to talk to someone, I try Matthew's cell phone number but just get the message service. I don't want to leave a message. So then I try his house, since I'm thinking he might just be hanging out and have his cell phone off. But his mom answers and says he's not home.

"Oh." I'm trying to decide whether to leave a message or not.

"He's out playing golf with his grandfather," she says in a very uptight voice.

"We were going to do something today," I say, "but I had to go out. Just tell him I called, okay?"

"If I see him, which isn't likely. But I'll leave a note."

I thank her and hang up. Then, still feeling kind of stunned by the events of this afternoon, I just walk around the house in a bit of a stupor. I try to pray again, but the words are choppy and stilted, and I don't even know what to say. Then I try to play my violin, but even that feels all wrong. Finally I sit in front of my computer and attempt to answer some letters.

Dear Jamie,
    I'm fifteen and have a part-time job and feel that I'm pretty responsible when it comes to money. I think I'm old enough to have my own credit card, but my parents said "forget it." I told them that it would help me to learn about finances, but they just don't get it. They say I'm too young and that I'll mess up. What do you think?
    No Credit

Okay, here's what I really think.

Dear No Credit,
    Get real. Your parents are right. You are too young. Get over it.
    Just Jamie

Okay, I won't write that. In fact, I won't write anything today. I just can't.

Twelve

Thursday, June 6

I feel like I'm losing it. Like I can feel life or time or something important just slipping through my fingers, like I can't really hang on. It's hard to describe, and I can't even wrap my head around it, except that it feels totally out of character—it's not like me to be like this.

I think I first started feeling seriously whacked on that day I took Nat to Haven and assumed she was getting an abortion. But I guess I sort of brushed it aside when I realized she hadn't actually done it (yet), telling myself I would deal with it later. Then I fell apart when I heard from Matthew the next day on Tuesday.

"Sorry, I didn't call yesterday," he told me. "I went with my grandpa to play golf, and it kind of turned into an all-day thing."

"That's okay." Of course, I don't mention that he could've called me later that evening.

"We had a really great time, and we were just finishing up the sixteenth hole when Grandpa got this idea about taking me to Europe as a graduation present. He was talking about all the galleries and museums and how it would be good for my art."

"Wow."

"Yeah, that's what I was thinking. So anyway, we finished up golf and went to his house and got online, and he started looking for good travel deals. And you're not going to believe this, Kim; he actually booked a trip."

"That's cool."

"We leave on Thursday. Can you believe it?"

"Seriously? You're leaving this Thursday?"

"Yeah. Grandpa got a great deal because we were able to just pick up and go."

"How long will you be gone?"

"We're not really sure. I mean, the round-trip ticket isn't booked until early August, but Grandpa said we could change our plans if we wanted."

"That's like two months," I said, surprised that I could actually do the math since I've been feeling so brain-dead.

"Yeah. But Grandpa thinks it'll take that long to really see what we need to see. It'll be hard being away from you that long, Kim, but this is such a great opportunity for me—and for my art, you know? I couldn't say no."

"Of course not, Matthew. This is incredible. I'm so happy for you." But even as I said this, I felt tears building up and I could hear the gruffness in my throat.

"I, uh, I have to go right now. I promised Nat that I'd help her with something." Okay, that was a lie, but I had to get off the phone.

"I've got a bunch of stuff to do too. Lucky for me, I already have a passport. Grandpa's picking me up in few minutes to take care of some of the other details." So we said good-bye and hung up, and I began to cry again.

It seems like I've been crying for days now—almost as much as I did right after Mom died. And while I know I'm crying for missing her, I'm also crying for something else too. I'm just not sure what exactly. It's probably a bunch of things—like knowing I'll miss Matthew this summer, plus this whole nasty thing with Natalie.

Get a grip, Kim. Just chill. But it's like I can't. I just pace around the house or else sleep. I've been sleeping a lot during the day. Then I end up awake at night, and I walk around the dark, quiet house and just cry. And when I try to pray, the words get stuck. I feel like everything in me is all stopped up.

Matthew came by last night to say good-bye. He didn't have time for much more than that. And I suppose that was a good thing since I was pretty much falling apart.

"I'm sorry," he told me as we hugged. "Don't take it so hard, Kim. I'll be back before you know it. And I'll write every day."

"I'm sorry." I tried to hold back the tears. "I think I'm just extra emotional right now. There's a lot of stuff going on in my life. I'm really glad for you—glad for this opportunity. It's so cool, Matthew. I hope you have a great time."

He smiled down at me. "Thanks, Kim. Maybe we can do this trip together someday. I'll know my way around, and I can show you all the best places."

I nodded, but somehow I knew this was never going to happen. Still, I pretended as if I believed it would, as if I believed that life was really going to get better for me.

Today, as Matthew was flying to Frankfurt, I was sleeping. I think I slept most of the day. Now it's nighttime, and I'm guessing he's in Germany by now. So far away. I feel so far away. So lost.

Friday, June 7

I get up this morning and tell myself that I'm going to snap out of this—whatever cloud of gloom and doom that's hanging over my head. I tell myself that I'm going to go outside and look at the flowers and trees, that I'm going to smell the air and listen to the birds—just like Mom told me to do in that letter. But it is nearly noon by the time I get up, and I don't feel like doing anything. I don't even shower or get dressed. And I don't feel like eating.

Instead I plop myself down on the couch, turn on the TV, and make myself into a vegetable as I watch one soap opera after another. I remind myself of Aunt Shannon. Although I don't think I'm actually listening or focusing much, but finally there is this one scene where a young woman is talking about losing a baby and how she's been depressed. I think about Natalie, and I just want to scream.

How can she seriously want to do this? What has happened to her? I turn off the TV, toss down the remote, and start pacing again. Okay, I know it's not my decision and not really my business, but it just gets me that she can change like this. Like one day it's a horrible sin to kill an unborn baby, and the next day it's okay.

Before I really know what I'm doing, I have walked down to her house in my pajamas (which are actually boxer shorts and a tank top), and I am knocking on her door—ready for a confrontation.

Fortunately Krissy and Micah are at day camp so Natalie is alone. And before I have time to really think this thing out or plan my words, I am staging an all-out assault on Natalie. Throwing the same kind of pro-life words at her that she once threw at me.

"It's not the baby's fault." I continue my sermon, not letting her get a word in edgewise as she sits on the edge of the couch, her hands in tight fists, as if she'd like to punch me. "He or she has no choice in this matter. And yet you're willing to just snuff that life out so you'll look good and can preserve your pride, your good little Christian girl image. But how are you going to feel," I say, "when the day comes and you have to stand before God and account for killing that innocent baby? How are you going to feel when the whole world knows what you've done, Natalie? Sure, you might be able to sweep this under the carpet now, but one day it's going to be shouted from the rooftops, and how will you feel then?"

Okay, now I know I've gone too far. I've reduced my friend to tears, and I know that I've said way too much, and none of it in love. It's like I'm just venting to make myself feel better. But the problem is, I now feel horrible. I feel like a failure and the worst friend on the planet. I can't imagine what Jamie would say to someone as heartless and selfish as I have just been. God, what is wrong with me?

My legs are shaking as I stand there watching Natalie crying. I know I should go over and hug her and tell her I'm sorry and that I'm so stupid and I just happen to be having a personal meltdown myself, but instead I turn away and walk out. I just leave her like that—a pile of pain I helped to create. I make myself sick. In fact, I feel physically sick as I walk toward my house. I'm getting that same weird tingling and numbing sensation I got on Monday, after we came home from the women's clinic.

By the time I get into the house, my hands and feet are completely numb. Even my nose and lips are numb. And now my ears are ringing really loudly, and my heart is racing and I'm sure that I'm about to die. Probably God's judgment on me for being such a jerk. I deserve it. But I sit down and wait, hoping that this crud will pass. But it doesn't. I only feel worse.

I stand up and walk around now, still numb and tingly, and my heart is racing and pounding like I've just finished a marathon. I am getting seriously freaked. Something is really wrong with me, and I don't know what to do.

I consider going online to see if there's some explanation for these weird symptoms, and I vaguely remember hearing about allergic reactions that cause numbness and eventually block your airways. And maybe I'm being obsessive or even a hypochondriac, but I am really, really worried. Finally, I don't know what to do. I consider calling Natalie, but after my tongue-lashing, how can I? Matthew is gone. And so, in final desperation, I call my dad.

I quickly describe my frightening symptoms, and he tells me to call 9-1-1.

"No way, Dad," I tell him, trying to calm myself, trying to just breathe. "It's not that bad. I don't want an ambulance. It's just very weird, and I don't know what to do. But I can't call—"

"Okay, I'm going to hang up and call you right back on my cell phone. Then I'm driving home, and I want you to stay on the line until I get there, understand? If you don't, I will call 9-1-1."

I agree, and feeling even more freaked at his reaction, I follow his directions, keeping the phone with me as I get a glass of water and take a few sips. Then I go lie down on the couch and wait. My dad's voice is so soothing and calming I actually feel better by the time he gets home. Maybe this whole thing was just my imagination.

"I'm sorry," I tell him, sitting up. "It's probably nothing."

"Get in the car," he commands as he helps me to my feet. "My secretary called ahead to Dr. Grier, and they'll be expecting you."

So it is that I find myself being examined by our family doctor, and there in his office, trusting his confidentiality, I break down and tell him everything—everything from how much I miss my mom and my boyfriend, to how my best friend is pregnant and how I just laid into her about her choice to get an abortion.

As I'm going on and on about this, he is checking all my vital signs and listening and nodding and commenting when it's appropriate. Finally, it seems the exam is over.

"Am I gonna make it, Doc?" I ask, hoping to sound much lighter than I feel.

"You're under a lot of stress, Kim."

I nod, blinking back more tears.

"That's a huge load for anyone to carry…"

"I know."

"So, what can you do to change anything?" he asks as he writes some things down on a chart. I'm thinking he's prescribing some form of psychiatric care for me. Maybe they'll lock me up.

"I don't know…" I try to think of an answer. "Usually, I try to pray about stuff like this, but lately it hasn't worked. It's like I've been so stressed that I can't even pray. It's like I'm stuck."

"Maybe God is trying to tell you something."

I study him for a moment. To be honest, I didn't even know that Dr. Grier believed in God. "What?" I finally ask.

"I'm not sure. But maybe He's trying to get your attention. Maybe He wants you to see that you're taking on too much. For instance, with your friend who's pregnant, doesn't she have anyone else she can lean on?"

I sadly shake my head. "No. She won't even tell her mom."

"Too bad." He presses his lips together, as if thinking, then tells me that he's going to talk to my dad while I get dressed.

I consider asking him about patient-doctor privilege since I don't want Dad to know about Nat's pregnancy. But why bother? Why must I keep Natalie's secret from my own dad? It's not like he'll tell anyone.

By the time I leave the examining room, the doctor has a prescription waiting for me, some kind of antianxiety medication I'm not sure I even want to take. And according to the nurse, he and Dad are still "in conference."

Finally, they come out and Dr. Grier pats me on the back. "You have an extraordinary daughter, Allen."

Dad nods. "I know that."

Then we leave, but we're barely in the car when I start grilling Dad for details.

"Dr. Grier and I both agree you are under too much stress, Kim."

I nod. "Yeah, I guess that's true."

"And so I've made a decision."

I turn and look at my dad. "What do you mean?"

"I mean, I'm sending you on a vacation."

"Huh?"

So he explains how he'd called his mother last weekend, worried that I might possibly be pregnant. "But she was off playing bingo," he continues. "So she called me back on Monday, and I explained that things were under control now. But she really wanted me to send you out for a visit. At the time it seemed unnecessary, and I told her as much. But now, after this little breakdown—"

"Breakdown?"

"Well, that's not exactly right. Dr. Grier said it was most likely a panic or anxiety attack. Too much stress probably ignited the whole thing, and as a result you started having physical symptoms. It's your body's way of telling you that you're putting yourself through too much. Anyway, I think it would be good for you to stay with your grandma—"

"And the alligators?"

Dad sort of chuckles. "Oh, I'm sure you'll keep a safe distance from the gators, Kim. But being at her place, where life is quiet and slow and easy, I think it might be good for you. And it's just what the doctor ordered."

"Grandma and the alligators?" I say again, dumbfounded. "You gotta be kidding."

"Just think about it."

So that's what I've been doing all night long—just thinking about it. And this is only making me feel worse. I think I'm having a serious meltdown here. It's like I'm unable to reason, I can't think straight, and I can't get my feelings under control. Even my prayers are pathetic, just hopeless cries for help, with no faith involved. I'm a mess.

Finally, it's nearly midnight, and I decide that maybe Dr. Grier is right, so I will take one of those little pills. I don't like the idea of using chemicals to "feel better," but I don't like the idea of losing my mind either. And right now it feels as if it could be one or the other. <u>God, help me</u>. That's about the only prayer I can pray at the moment. I hope He's listening.

Thirteen

Monday, June 10

Despite my mental stability, or lack of it, I did go to church yesterday. Although I didn't go to youth group on Saturday. I didn't want to see Ben and end up lashing out at him for getting Nat pregnant and disrupting our lives. And I knew I couldn't trust myself, or my out-of-control emotions, <u>not</u> to do that. But going to church did make me feel slightly better, at least during the worship time.

Then I happened to notice Ben O'Conner sitting up front, and I got to thinking about this whole unborn baby dilemma again. Was it fair for Natalie to make this life-or-death decision without Ben even knowing he could be a father? I mean, don't dads have any rights?

Then Pastor Tony got up to speak, and I realized that he and Steph would be relatives of this unborn baby as well—and yet they would never know—they would

never have a chance to express an opinion. It just seems
so wrong that one person is allowed to snuff out a life
like that—without consulting anyone. It just gets me.

I mean, I realize that Nat's got a lot on the line here. I
know that going through a full-term pregnancy will be
extremely hard on her. But in the long run, it might be
just as hard on her to abort her baby. Especially as I
consider how Natalie has struggled with huge guilt over
losing her virginity. That threw her into a total tailspin.
What will happen to her if she aborts her baby and then
regrets it and feels guilty?

So even though I didn't focus too much on Pastor
Tony's sermon, I did come home with a plan. And that
was to talk to Natalie. First of all, I would apologize for
acting like such a jerk on Friday. Then I would ask her to
consider these things.

I called first to make sure she was home. And I
wasn't surprised when she hung up on me. As I walked
to her house, I could tell by the car in the driveway that
her mom was there, and that was probably a good thing
because Natalie would be forced to act civilized and
she'd have to listen to me.

"Nat's in her room," Mrs. McCabe tells me after she
opens the door. She's still dressed in "church" clothes
and appears to have her hands full with Krissy and
Micah, who are both whining about not getting to go to
McDonald's for lunch.

I don't bother knocking on the door since I know
Natalie will only tell me to go away.

"Look," I say as I slip into her room. "I come in peace, okay? I just want to tell you I'm really, really sorry for the way I acted on Friday. I don't blame you if you don't forgive me, but I want you to know that I totally blew it, and I'm really sorry."

She is sitting like a stone on her bed, just staring at me with the angriest expression I've ever seen across her face.

I pull out a chair and sit down. "If it makes you feel any better, I went home and had this, well, sort of like a breakdown or meltdown or anxiety attack. My dad had to come home and take me to the doctor."

Now her anger seems to lift a bit, and she looks slightly curious.

"He said it's because of stress, and he prescribed some pills, and he and my dad cooked up this plan to get me away—for a mental-health break."

"No way."

"It's true. Dad is ready to ship me off to my grandma's."

She frowns now. "Are you serious?"

I nod. I don't tell her that I actually agreed to this lame plan. I'll save that for later.

"Your crazy grandma in Florida?"

I nod again. "She's been feeding the alligators lately."

"Isn't that illegal?"

"Yeah." I take in a deep breath. "But I was in church today, and well, I saw Ben there, and I got to thinking, Nat. Shouldn't he have a say in this? I mean, he's the father…doesn't he have any rights?"

"Not legally."

Okay, I know she's right about this. I did some quick research online, and as it is, the father of an unborn child has no say in the termination of a pregnancy. Even if the couple is married! I think that's pretty weird. "I know legally he can't oppose an abortion, but don't you think it's interesting that he would have to pay child support if you had the child? I mean, doesn't that seem unfair?"

"Is it fair that I would have to give up nine months of my life, my reputation, my education, my sanity, probably my home…and he just gets to go about as if nothing has happened?"

I just shake my head. "I guess fair isn't the right word. And I do get your point. It doesn't seem fair." I consider my next point. "Okay, I thought about something else at church, Nat. This has more to do with you personally, okay, I mean your well-being."

"What?" Her voice has that flatness to it now, like she really doesn't want to hear this. And maybe she doesn't, but I need to say it.

"Well, I remember how you fell apart about losing your virginity. It's like you were on a one-way guilt trip straight to hell. And I'm thinking, okay, if you have that much guilt over a virginity pledge, how are you going to feel about taking a human life? I mean, later on when you have time to really think about it. Isn't it going to hurt?"

"You know, Kim, I don't really need this right now.

You might think you're helping me, but you aren't."

"I know it's not easy to think about this—"

"I think about it all the time, Kim. It's all I think about. And all I can think is I either end this pregnancy or I end my life. What would you recommend?"

This stumps me. "Counseling?"

She makes a growling sound. "Yeah, you and my stupid mom. But I don't want counseling. I just want to end this. And if I had a pill that I could take, one that would stop this pregnancy, I wouldn't even think about it; I would take it right now."

Okay, I'm at a loss for words. I don't know why ever I thought that Nat would be reasonable about this. I suppose I assumed that if I remained calm and controlled, she would too. Looks like once again, I was wrong.

"I'm sorry," I tell her.

"Yeah, me too." But her tone is not apologetic. Just mad.

"And I, uh, I won't be able to take you to Haven on Wednesday."

She looks slightly frightened now. "What? What do you mean?"

"I mean, my dad has booked a flight to Florida for me. I leave Tuesday morning."

Natalie looks like I just punched her in the stomach. "No, Kim," she says in a low desperate voice. "You can't leave yet. Can't you just change the flight? Until like Thursday? Please, I really need you to be here for this."

There's a huge lump in my throat now. "I'm sorry, Nat. It's all set."

"But, Kim—" She starts to cry.

"I'm sorry," I say, standing. I just want to leave. I can't stand to see her looking so helpless and desperate.

"What will I—?"

"I don't know, Nat." I'm reaching for the door and experiencing those same feelings I had on Friday—heart pounding, tingling, and it feels like I could barf. "I'm sorry," I say again. And then I leave.

When I get home, I slip to my room without talking to my dad. I get into bed and I cry and cry. Finally I get up and take one of those stupid pills. And then I sleep for the rest of the afternoon. I am pathetic.

Tuesday, June 11

I am on my way to Florida right now. Row 27, seat B. Dad made me take one of those pills just before we said good-bye at the security gates.

"Dr. Grier made me promise," he told me as he handed me a bottle of water to wash it down with. "He said that would ensure an anxiety-free flight."

I nodded, trying to hold back the tears.

"You're going to be okay, Kim."

"Are you sure this is a good idea, Dad?" I asked for like the tenth time since Sunday.

He reached out and took me in his arms. "I think it

is. I'm so busy at work right now and I've been so, well, distracted, I'm not much good for you. And all the stress that's on you…"

"Yeah," I agreed as I clung to him. "You're probably right. But remember your promise, Dad. If it doesn't work out, if I don't like it there, I can come home, right?"

"You can come home as soon as you like, Kimmy. But for your grandma's sake, and for Uncle Garth, I hope you can stay at least a week. It would mean so much to them."

"I know…" He let go of me, and I stepped back and looked at him. I swear he's aged about twenty years during the past six months. And I'm sure my problems aren't helping.

"I think you'll be surprised at how easygoing they are. Quirky, yes, but their lifestyle is really simple and peaceful." He looked almost wistful as he said this.

"What if I get stressed out by Grandma feeding her alligators?" I teased, hoping to lighten things up.

He shook his head. "I already told her to stop that. She knows it's illegal. But she's just like that sometimes, Kimmy. Still, she's got a good heart. I know you're going to enjoy her." Then we said our final good-bye, I got in line and waved one last time, and I was on my way.

And I'm thinking that pill must've helped because I really don't feel too uptight right now. And I'm sitting here, sipping a Sierra Mist and getting to know this computer—Dad gave me his old laptop. He said he was due for an upgrade anyway, and he knew that Grandma didn't have one. "That way we can keep in touch through e-mail," he assured me. "Of course, feel free to call if you like."

And so as I'm sitting here, feeling amazingly calm, I'm thinking maybe this won't be so bad after all. Maybe Dad and Dr. Grier were right. This "vacation" might be a good distraction for me. Hopefully it will keep me from obsessing over Natalie—and the baby. That just hurts too much. I know that it's more than I can handle right now. I have to let it go.

I told Dad I wanted to continue doing my column while I'm in Florida, and that it's one of the few things about my life that makes me feel better. I think it's almost therapeutic. That's probably because it gives me a sense of control—even if it's only an illusion. But I can imagine that my responses are helping someone—that some kids are paying attention and making better choices.

Oh, sure, I was blocked up there for a day or two, but that's only because the stress levels were getting to me. But I think I can handle it when things settle down. And since I've got some time to spare, I decided to answer some letters during my flight to Florida.

Dear Jamie,
    I've never had a boyfriend, and I'm sure I never will. Boys just don't seem to be attracted to me. Do you think there's something wrong with me? Is there

anything you can suggest for me to do, something that will make boys notice me more? I'll be thirteen in July, and I've never even been kissed.

Hopeless

Dear Hopeless,

I didn't have my first kiss until I was nearly sixteen, and even then it wasn't anything to brag about. I don't get why you're feeling so desperate so soon. Have you been reading the wrong books or watching too many grown-up shows on TV? Why don't you give yourself a break and just have fun being twelve going on thirteen and let this whole boy thing wait a few years? Think about this—you only have a short amount of time to be a kid, and after that you have to be an adult for the rest of your life. Enjoy it while it's here. Because before you know it, it'll be gone.

Just Jamie

Fourteen

Tuesday, June 11

It was about five o'clock (Florida time) when my final
flight landed in Naples. According to Dad, Grandma and
Uncle Garth would be down at baggage claim to pick me
up. But I started to feel nervous. What if they didn't
show? Or what if they're so weird that it's freaky to stay
with them? Or what if the alligators were crawling all
over the place? Or what if my bags were lost? Or what
if—shut up, Kim! Quit obsessing before you have a
panic attack! I considered taking another one of those
pills but decided not to. I really should be able to gut this
out.

I followed the directions to baggage claim but didn't
see anyone who quite fit the description of Grandma or
Uncle Garth—and I'm thinking they should stand out in a
crowd. But after a brief wait, I was relieved to see my

bright red bag going around the carousel. I grabbed it and went over by the door to wait.

After about fifteen minutes, I was feeling nervous again. I considered calling Dad on my cell phone, but then I didn't want to worry him unnecessarily. Plus I knew that out-of-state phone calls would be expensive. So I just waited.

Finally, I saw this older dude in a Hawaiian shirt, raggedy cargo shorts, rubber flip-flops, and a beat-up cowboy hat coming my way. "Kim?" he said hopefully.

"Yeah?" I didn't say his name, just in case this was an imposter who'd shown up to abduct me. I'd only seen a couple photos of my uncle, and they were taken when he was younger. I think he's supposed to be in his forties now, but I wasn't totally sure this was the guy.

"I'm your uncle," he said with a bright smile. "Uncle Garth." He reached out and shook my hand.

I nodded, still feeling a bit unsure.

"Mom, I mean, Grandma, is out in the car. Her feet are still bugging her since her operation, so it's hard for her to walk too far."

Okay, now I'm thinking this must be Uncle Garth. Besides, those fine creases by his eyes remind me of Dad. "Thanks for picking me up," I said, feeling a little lame for being such a chicken.

"No problem. We're just glad you finally came to visit. But you're all grown up now, Kimmy."

I kind of laughed. "It's been a while, huh?"

"Yeah, I think you were still wearing diapers when

you guys came to visit." He took my bag for me. "Hey, I'm sorry about your mom. That's a real bummer."

"Yeah," I said as we went outside. "Thanks."

It's hot and humid out here, but it felt surprisingly good. I don't even know why, but for some reason I liked it. Before long we stopped by this old peach-colored Cadillac that's as big as a boat.

"Kimmy!" Grandma got out of the backseat of the car and grabbed me by both arms and just looked at me. "I can hardly believe it's you. Why look how grown-up you look." Then she pinched my cheek. "But you're not very tall, and you're a little on the thin side." She laughed. "But that's okay; I can fatten you up."

Now while I'm feeling flattered that she thought I was thin, I wasn't too sure about the "fatten you up" part. "Thanks for coming to get me," I said as I studied her strange outfit of a print dress with tropical flowers the size of dinner plates, over a pair of coral-colored pants, topped with a large pink straw hat that's decorated with fake pieces of fruit. One slightly swollen foot had on a low-heeled white sandal, and the other was wearing a bright blue medical wrap. "I forgot about your feet and everything. I hope this wasn't hard on you."

"Oh, that's no big deal. I just ride in the backseat and keep them propped up. One foot seems to have healed up just fine and dandy, but this dad-burned right foot is still troubling me some. The doc might have to do another operation on it. But I don't mind getting out for a drive. I enjoy the scenery. Get tired of being housebound all the time."

Uncle Garth had already put my stuff in the trunk. "Y'all ready?"

"I'm ready when you are." Grandma hoisted herself into the backseat, and I got into the front.

"I really don't remember much about your place," I said as my uncle started to back up. "I guess I was pretty small the last time I was here."

"Well, not much has changed," Grandma said from behind me. "At least not much on my property. But the town's gotten bigger."

"How big is Port City?" The only reason I remembered the name of the town was because Dad filled me in a little right before I left.

"Goodness' sakes, I think the population is nearly up to two thousand now," Grandma said.

I tried not to laugh since that sounded pretty small to me.

"They just got a new grocery store complex, and it's got some other stores with it. Very modern," she continued. "And I hear they may put in a traffic light next year."

"Are you still feeding the alligators?" I asked.

She laughed. "Well, that's our little secret now, isn't it, Kimmy? Your daddy gave me a lecture about it and I told him I'd consider his point of view. But it's hard to teach an old dog new tricks, don't you think?"

Soon we're on the open road, and Uncle Garth was

driving like there were no speed limit. I tried to see the speedometer and thought it was close to ninety. I was glad I fastened my seatbelt, although I was surprised to see that he hadn't. I'm sure that my fingernails were digging gouges into the old velvet upholstery, and I wanted to ask my uncle to slow down, but I wasn't sure I should say anything. So to my surprise I actually started to pray. It's the first time I'd prayed in a week, but I asked God to keep us safe and to help get me through this visit. Suddenly I wasn't sure what I'd gotten myself into.

Somehow we made it to Grandma's place without a ticket or a wreck. I was so relieved to get out of that Caddy that I found I was chatting away with both Grandma and Uncle Garth, nervous chatter I suppose, but they didn't seem to notice as we went inside.

Grandma's property was very unique. She owned forty acres, "give or take," about a mile out of town. Uncle Garth actually slowed down to the speed limit as he drove through bustling Port City, and they did, indeed, have a new strip mall, complete with about six businesses. Big times. Why they needed a traffic light was a mystery to me.

But back to Grandma's place. Her house was what I'd describe as a bungalow, although I wasn't even sure why. It had weathered wood siding and a metal roof, kind of hillbilly looking. It's built low and compact, and its best feature, in my opinion, was the wide wrap-around screened-in porch. Grandma said I can sleep out

here if I like. She told me it was built in the twenties.
She and my grandpa (who died before I was born)
bought it in the sixties, shortly after my dad graduated
from college. They added plumbing and a few, <u>very</u>
<u>few</u>, amenities.

After my brief tour, she told me, "If you run too
much electrical gadgets at once, you'll blow a fuse." She
doesn't have TV, and the phone looks like something
from an old movie. "Don't have much use for the
telephone," she said when I examined it. Thankfully, Dad
already set up the laptop for wireless, although he
warned me that I might have to go outside and search
for a place to get a connection.

"Want to see my place now?" Uncle Garth asked after
I put my stuff in my room, which is about ten by ten and
in the back of the house.

I said, "Sure," and he took me down a narrow trail
where I kept my eyes peeled for alligators. We went
about fifty yards from Grandma's house, and beyond
some overgrown vegetation was an old caboose that
had been remodeled into living quarters.

"How did this get here?" I asked, seeing that there
were no train tracks.

"My dad bought it at an auction when I was a kid,
and a big old truck brought it out here. We had to cut a
road special, but the plants have all grown back so you
can't hardly tell."

"And this is where you live?" I asked as we went
inside the strange abode.

"Yep. Dad and me fixed it all up, even ran electricity from the house so I can have lights."

I looked around the crowded quarters, and other than clutter, the place was pretty neat and tidy. "It's cozy."

"Yeah, I like it."

"So what do you do?" I asked him. Now my dad already explained how his younger brother sustained some brain damage during birth, how he never developed beyond about a twelve-year-old academically, and how his parents took him out of school after sixth grade. "But he's a good guy," Dad said, "with a kind heart. And he's made something of a life for himself."

"Oh, I like to fish and stuff," Uncle Garth said, "and I make things."

"What kind of things?"

So he showed me his workshop, a smaller building that was just behind the caboose. "I'm working on this table right now." He showed me a rustic-looking table. "This is pine." He rubbed his hand over the top. "I love the smell of pine." Then he picked up a tool and began running it over the wood.

"What are you doing?"

"Planing," he told me. "This is a plane and it smoothes the wood. You see?"

I ran my hand over the wood. "Yeah, that's nice."

"Well, I guess I'll work now. You can watch if you want."

So I sat on a stool, one that I'm sure he must've

made, and I watched him for nearly an hour. And as I sat there, I felt as if I'd gone back in time. But then I heard a bell ringing, and Uncle Garth said that meant supper was ready. So we headed back to the house.

"Your dad just called," Grandma told me as we went inside.

"Everything okay?"

"He just wanted to make sure your flight went well."

"Fried chicken," Uncle Garth said as he rubbed his hands together.

"Does that mean the alligators will be dropping by later?" I whispered so Grandma wouldn't hear. I didn't want to encourage her.

He laughed. But I was actually somewhat serious. So far I hadn't seen a gator, but I was worried they could be lurking nearby.

"Have a seat." Grandma set a pitcher of iced tea on the table.

"Can I help?" I offered, suddenly realizing that she was hobbling around on her bad foot.

"Yes," she said in relief. "You fetch that pot of greens. And Garth, you get that platter of chicken out of the oven." And then she sat down and sighed, giving us orders for putting the food on the table. Finally, everything seemed to be satisfactory, and we all sat down, and my uncle bowed his head and blessed the food. To my surprise his words sounded very sincere, not some recited blessing, but the prayer seemed to come from his heart.

"I haven't seen any alligators yet," I ventured as we
began to eat.

"I should hope not," said Grandma as she passed the
"greens." I still wasn't too sure what they were, but I
took a cautious serving.

"The gators don't come up here," said Uncle Garth.

"That's right," said Grandma. "They stick close to the
water."

"Where's that?" For some reason it seemed
important to establish where these alligators actually
lived, especially before I went to bed tonight. I didn't
want to lie there imagining an alligator slithering into the
house uninvited.

"It's about half a mile away," said Grandma. "Too far
for me to walk with these feet of mine. But I take out
Old Nellie, and we get there just fine."

"Old Nellie?" I couldn't quite imagine my grandma
on a horse.

"A golf cart," said Uncle Garth. "Mom's wheels."

"Oh."

"We've got lots of wheels 'round here," said
Grandma. "If you get a hankering to take a drive, you
can have your pick, Kimmy."

I wasn't sure that I wanted to drive that big Cadillac
just yet, but maybe if I got desperate enough.

I offered to clean up after dinner, and Grandma didn't
protest. Of course, I quickly learned that she doesn't
have any conveniences like a dishwasher or garbage
disposal. But she sat in her chair with her feet propped

up and explained the workings of her old-fashioned kitchen.

"Don't put those chicken scraps in the compost bucket," she said.

"The garbage then?" I called back.

"Well, uh, I guess so."

So I dropped them in the garbage can under the sink, but I noticed that she retrieved them later, putting them into a recycled plastic sack in the bottom of the refrigerator, so I'm guessing she hasn't given up her illegal activities just yet.

"I usually don't turn in quite this early," she told me as she started hobbling off to her bedroom. "But I reckon I'm a little worn out. I hope you don't mind, Kimmy."

"Of course not. I've got some things to keep me busy."

So after she went to bed, I took my laptop out to the porch to see if I could get any wireless service. But even after trying it from every angle, it just wasn't connecting. And because it was dark and I was still feeling uneasy about the alligator population, I decided not to venture out.

I just sat on the screened porch for a while, listening to the weird sounds all around me. I'm guessing it was frogs and crickets, and well, I'm not entirely sure. I wished I could go online and find out what kind of animals live in these parts, because I got to thinking that besides alligators, which still unnerve me, there could also be snakes and who knows what else.

I also wished I could go online to communicate with my dad. I really wanted to talk to him. I even turned on my cell phone, thinking one expensive call might be worth it, but it, too, had no connection. Talk about feeling isolated. It's like I was all alone on some deserted island. I even considered using my grandma's phone but didn't want to do it without asking first.

Finally, I felt too spooked to be out on the porch by myself. I imagined big spiders or other insects crawling around in the darkness, and I knew I needed to get inside the house before I really started to panic. I turned off the one light in the living room and instantly wished I hadn't. Now the entire house was pitch-black. I felt along the wall to the hallway and finally to my room and was so relieved to turn on a light again.

This room used to be Uncle Garth's, my grandma told me earlier. "Now I mostly use it to store my seashell collection." The wood-paneled walls of this tiny room are painted in sky blue, and pine shelves (made by my uncle) filled with hundreds of seashells hang on most of the walls. It's really kind of cool looking, in a funky way.

Other than that, there is a twin-sized bed with a metal headboard painted white. The bed is topped with a faded patchwork quilt—"a crazy quilt," Grandma explained. "My mother made it for me when I was about twelve. Some of these scraps came from dresses I

wore when I was a little girl." There's also a small pine
dresser right next to the bed, a painted wooden chair, a
tiny closet, and a window with a white curtain trimmed
in lace.

At first I wasn't too impressed with the room, but it
started to grow on me as I quietly put my things away
and did a quick spider and bug check. I even checked
the window screen to make sure it was secure, since
Grandma informed me that the only way to cool the
house is to have the windows open at night. Finally, I
was satisfied. I sat on the slightly squeaky bed and was
surprised to see that it wasn't even ten o'clock yet. And I
was not the least bit tired.

I was desperately trying not to think about Natalie,
trying to block out what she intended to do tomorrow.
Just the thought of her at the Haven Women's Clinic
made me feel physically ill. It's overwhelming.
Frightening. I tried to pray for her, and I even asked God
to stop her from this foolishness, but the words felt
stilted and false. Not nearly as sincere as Uncle Garth's
simple blessing at dinner. Could I be losing my faith?

Finally, I could tell I was obsessing and getting so
wound up that I'd never be able to go to sleep tonight.
So when I went to the bathroom to brush my teeth, I
also took one of the antianxiety pills. I hoped it would
work.

Then I decided to answer some letters for my
column, just until I got sleepy. Maybe it would take my
mind off of Natalie.

Dear Jamie,

I really want to get a job this summer, but every place I apply at says I don't have any experience. But how do I get experience if no one will hire me? My best friend says I should just make something up, something that can't be traced. Do you think that's wrong? And if it's wrong, how do I get someone to hire me so I can get some experience?

No Experience

Dear NE,

I don't think you should lie about job experience. First of all, that would compromise your personal integrity, but besides that your employer might find out and you could have even more trouble finding another job. But maybe you have some kind of job experience that you've overlooked. Have you ever babysat, done yard work or housework, had a paper route? Have you volunteered? All those things could be considered "experience." And if you haven't done those things, maybe you should consider it so you will have experience. Or else just keep applying, but be honest. And before you know it you'll be working and probably wishing for a vacation.

Just Jamie

Of course, I think that's kind of funny since I now find myself on a somewhat unwanted "vacation" and was almost wishing I was working instead. I remembered the

job I had at the mall last summer, and while I
complained about it, I did like the routine as well as the
extra money. But then this column is an even better job.
And who knows where it might lead? Now if I could
only go to sleep.

Fifteen

Thursday, June 13

Talk about antsy. I was a basket case for most of the day yesterday. I tried to appear interested in Grandma's little golf cart tour that eventually took us to the slough where she proceeded to toss out chicken scraps for her gators.

"This is the wrong time of day," she informed me. "But if we come back later, just after suppertime, we'll probably see Bill and Gloria. And maybe even Mr. Farley, although he's usually late—which is why I named him after my postman."

After that, Uncle Garth took me bird-watching. And I actually took some photos and tried to appear interested, but all I could think about was Natalie. I kept looking at my watch and trying to figure the time change. Had she gone into Haven? Had she had the abortion? Could there have been any complications? And even if it had gone smoothly in a medical sense, would her heart ever get over this? Would she be scarred for life?

I kept wishing I'd never come here and that I was home where I could do something. Sure, life felt stressful there and I was sort of falling apart. But really, which is worse? Worrying about a friend when you're right by her side, or when you're a whole world apart? And it literally feels like I'm in another world. Not just because it's totally different than what I'm used to, but because I feel so disconnected. No matter where I went on my grandma's property, I could NOT get a decent connection. Not on my phone and not on my laptop. Finally I just couldn't take it anymore.

"You mentioned that I could borrow a car," I told Grandma in the afternoon. "And I need to go someplace where I can check my e-mail."

She looked confused. "Well, the postman has already delivered the mail, dear. He was on time for a change. But there wasn't anything for you."

So I attempted to bring my grandma into the era of twenty-first century technology until she seemed to finally get it. Or almost. I also explained how I had a job writing for Dad's paper and that it was imperative for me to remain in contact during my stay here.

"Help yourself to a vehicle," she said. "There's my car or the pickup, and I'm sure Garth wouldn't mind if you used his rig. In fact, he might be heading to town anyway. Maybe you'd like him to give you a ride." But it turned out Uncle Garth was finishing up a woodworking project that he'd promised to a friend.

So I take the pickup, an ancient Willys Jeep with the hardest ride I've ever experienced. By the time I reach Port City, my insides feel like a bowl of jelly. But I soon discover that it's worth the trip, since both my cell phone and computer now work. First off, I get myself a big Lemon Coke, and then I walk across the street to the city park where I locate a small vacant table.

Then I turn on my laptop and read my e-mail. I have one fairly long one from my dad. It's very sweet. And there are two e-mails from Matthew, which are rather brief, but at least it sounds like he's enjoying Italy—it sounds like there are dozens of art galleries in every town. There are two e-mails from poor Maya who sounds frustrated. It seems her mom's behavior is getting more and more bizarre—or else my cousin is stringing me along with an overly active imagination.

So I respond to these e-mails and let everyone know I am doing fine and having an interesting time in Florida, land of the gators. And then I decide to e-mail Natalie. Not that I thought she would be checking e-mail today, but I just figure it's a small way to let her know I'm thinking of her. Especially after our horrible good-bye a few days ago.

Then I turn off my computer and decide to walk around town and check things out a bit. Of course, that takes about five minutes. And by then I am feeling pretty antsy again. It's like I really need to find out what's going on with Nat before I return to my disconnected state at

Grandma's house. I just can't stop thinking—and worrying—about her.

Finally, I try calling Natalie at home. It's almost five o'clock, and even with the time difference, I'm thinking she should be home by now. Still, I'm not sure she will even pick up. Furthermore, I'm not entirely sure that I am ready to talk to her. What will I say? Just the same, I return to my table in the small city park, sit down, and dial her number. And to my surprise, she answers.

"Nat! You're home."

"Yeah," she says without the slightest trace of enthusiasm. "Where'd you think I'd be?"

"Oh, I don't know…it's just so good to hear your voice."

"Where are you?"

"In Port City. It's the nearest town to my grandma's place. Man, she really lives out in the sticks."

"Seen any alligators?" Her voice still sounds pretty flat.

"Not yet." I pause, wondering what might be the best way to ask this next question. "How are you feeling today?"

"Like crud."

"So, uh, did you go to your appointment…?" I pause, but she doesn't say anything. "At Haven?" I add, as if she doesn't know what I'm talking about.

She sighs. "No."

"No?" I feel a faint ripple of hope. Like maybe she's changed her mind.

There's a long silence, and finally she says, "Yeah, well, I guess I just wasn't ready yet."

"Oh."

"I called and talked to a nurse this morning, and she said it was okay to postpone the procedure for a while, until I'm ready, that is."

"Oh." My tiny wisp of relief evaporates into the humid sea air. And now I really don't know what to say.

"It would've been a lot easier if I had someone to go with me..."

"I'm sorry, Nat. But I tried to explain—"

"I know. I know. You're cracking up, losing your mind, whatever you want to call it. Well, you and me both, Kim! Only I don't get to run away from my problems like some people. I have to stay here and face them head-on."

Her words sting, but I decide not to react. What good would it do anyway? There's another long stretch of silence, and I finally tell her that I should go. "My dad said these out-of-state calls will be expensive, since I don't have the best service, you know? But I can e-mail you. In fact, I already did."

"Yeah, right." This feels like another slap in the face.

"Look," I say in a firmer voice. "I'm sorry I can't help you through this, Nat. But I just can't, okay. Besides, you know how I feel about your, uh, decision and everything. It's not like I'm much encouragement. In fact, I don't even see why you'd want me around right now."

"Because you're my best friend," she says in an

angry voice. "And you should be here for me, Kim."

"Sorry," I tell her, although I suspect that I don't sound very sorry since I'm actually quite irritated.

"You already said that."

"Well, I better go. Take care, Nat."

"Yeah. You too." But her voice is sharp as a knife as she says this, almost as if she'd rather be saying "Go swim with the alligators, you traitor!"

Then we hang up. And now I feel so angry I want to throw my phone onto the ground and stomp it to pieces. I want to scream and shout and pound my fists on something. But instead I just sit here with my jaw clenched, and I'm sure, my blood pressure rising. I can't believe Nat is acting like this. Like it's somehow <u>my</u> fault that she's in this stupid situation.

And crud, if she wants to talk about best friends being supportive, what about all the things I've gone through before and after Mom died? Other than Matthew, I was pretty much on my own. Oh, sure, she might've been there for me a couple of times. But most of the time she's been off having one great big pity party for herself! Where does she get off treating me like this anyway?

I realize it's time to head back now. Especially since I told Grandma I'd help her with supper. But I'm still fuming as I rattle and bounce down the road back to her house. But maybe the jolting trip is therapeutic since I feel slightly numb when I arrive. Although I'm not sure whether it's from the ride or my phone conversation with Nat.

I help Grandma get dinner ready without talking much. I guess I'm still upset, still obsessing over the way Nat's treating me. Then as we eat, I am still not talking much. Afterward, Uncle Garth helps to clear the table, then excuses himself out to his shop. I offer to clean up the kitchen, but Grandma says she'll keep me company.

"I can sit here and dry dishes." She takes a dishtowel and sits at the kitchen table, propping her bad foot up on a chair in front of her. I suppose I'm still being pretty quiet as I scrape and wash dishes, until finally, my grandma wants to know if something is wrong.

And to my surprise, I end up pouring out the whole story of Natalie, the pregnancy, her plan to have an abortion—everything. It's like my cork got popped or something. Even so, I'm thinking that Nat's story should be safe out here in the boonies—who's my grandma going to tell, the gators? Besides that, I'm still angry at Nat. Maybe I don't care who knows anymore.

"Poor Natalie," Grandma says as I toss a corn husk into the compost bucket.

"Poor Natalie?" I suppose I expected my own grandma to feel a little bit sorry for me.

"Well, that's a heavy load for a girl to carry. And you say she's keeping this burden to herself—she hasn't even told her mother or the father-to-be yet?"

"No. I keep telling her that she should. But she's afraid her mom will get upset, and she probably will. And the guy, the father-to-be, well, he doesn't even like Natalie anymore. He has another girlfriend."

"Poor Natalie." Grandma makes a tsk-tsk sound. "She must be feeling very lonely right now."

"But it's her own fault. I mean, I still feel pretty lonely too, after having my mom die, but Natalie doesn't even seem to notice or much care most of the time. She's so concerned with herself and her own problems—" And that's when I start to cry.

"Oh, Kimmy, dear." Grandma sets aside the plate she was drying and gets up and comes over and puts her arms around me. "Yes, I can see how that would make you feel bad. You needed your good friend to comfort you, and there she was off having her own set of worries. Goodness knows, that must've been hard on you."

"I was trying to be a good friend to her." I try to sniff back the tears. "But I guess I just don't know how to deal with it, the pregnancy and everything. And then this whole abortion thing, well, it's just so depressing and upsetting."

"Of course it is. That's a lot for any young person to deal with. Is Natalie quite sure she wants an abortion?" Grandma steps back and wipes my tears with her slightly damp dishtowel now.

I shrug. "I'm not really sure. I guess I felt hopeful when I heard she canceled her appointment today. But she says it's only because she's not ready yet—like she thinks she'll still go through with it, like it's my fault for not being there to help her."

"There was a time, Kimmy…" Grandma eases

herself back down in the kitchen chair and starts
speaking in the same voice she uses when she's telling
me something from the past, like how her mother made
that crazy quilt. "A time when I wished I could have an
abortion too."

I feel my eyes getting big—my grandma wanted an
abortion? "Why?" I ask suddenly. "Was it with Garth?" I'd
heard she had been getting kind of old when her second
son was born. Maybe she had suspected there would be
problems.

"No, not with Garth, dear. With your daddy."

"Really?"

She leans back in the chair, draping the dishtowel
across her knees. "Now your daddy doesn't know all of
this story, Kimmy. He knows a bit, but there are some
things…well, I just didn't think he needed to hear."

"What?" I ask as I continue to scrub a pot.

"Your daddy doesn't know that I wasn't married
when I became pregnant with him." She pauses as if
waiting for me to react, but I just listen. "You see, it was
war times, and your daddy's father had just enlisted in
the Navy. We were engaged at the time, and I was ready
and willing to get married, but Ronald was worried that
something might happen to him. He thought he might
come home missing a leg or an arm or maybe even his
mind, like what had happened to one of his good
friends. So for my sake, he wanted us to wait. And
although we decided to wait to get married, we didn't
wait to, well, I think you understand what I'm getting at,

Kimmy, dear. So it was that Ronald went off to the South Pacific, and I discovered I was in the family way."

"That must've been really hard," I say as I realize what she's saying. "I mean, back in those days especially."

She laughs. "Well, as surprising as it may sound, it wasn't so terribly unusual during the war years. Still, it was embarrassing, and folks did what they could to cover these things up. Naturally, I wrote to Ronald straight away, explaining what had happened. And he wrote right back promising me that we would get married during his next leave." She sighs as she begins to wipe the pot that I hand her. "But my dear Ronald was killed before he ever got a leave."

"Oh, no." I turn and look at her. "That must've been awful for you."

She nods. "Yes, it was terrible. I didn't tell anyone, except my mother, what had happened. Then I moved away from my hometown in Indiana before my family could be embarrassed by the situation. I wanted to get as far away as possible, so I looked at a map and decided on Miami. I got a train ticket and came down to Florida with less than a hundred dollars in my purse. I got a job and rented a room, and somehow I managed. Of course, I wore a wedding ring and told anyone who wanted to know that my baby's daddy, my husband, had been killed in the Pacific. And no one ever questioned this."

"That must've been so hard, Grandma."

"Life was hard for everyone during that time. But people helped each other. I think the war brought out the goodness in a lot of folks."

"So when did you marry Uncle Garth's dad?"

"Oh, that was some time later. By then I'd taken some secretarial training and had gotten a decent job that supported me and my boy. Your daddy was just starting high school when I met Sid. At first Allen didn't much like the idea of another man coming into the picture. But after a while, he saw what a truly good man Sid was, and he finally came to his senses. Now, I had never dreamed of having more children, goodness knows I was close to forty, but the Good Lord must've had other plans, because just a few years after I married Sid, little Garth came along." She sighs as she sets the dry pot aside. "And what a blessing that boy has been to me. A real comfort in my old age."

"He's a sweet guy." Still, as I drain the soapy water from the sink, I am feeling slightly stunned by this whole story. Who would've guessed that my own dad had been "born out of wedlock"? Maybe he and I have more in common than I realized.

"The only reason I'm telling you all this, Kimmy, is so that maybe you'll understand how it might feel to be in your friend's position. It's a very tough spot."

"But you said you had wished for an abortion, Grandma. Do you still feel that way?"

She laughs. "Of course not. It was just a moment of desperation that made me wish for that nonsense. And after I lost Ronald and Allen was born, well, I was so thankful to have that piece of Ronald still with me. Allen looks an awful lot like his father. Remind me to show you a photo sometime."

"So Dad knew that his father had died in the war, but you never told him that you weren't married?"

"Not that I'd mind if he knew, Kimmy; I've made my peace with all that. I just never saw the need to tell him."

Then Grandma announces that it's time to check on the gators. "You want to drive?" she asks as she hobbles outside to where Old Nellie is parked.

"Sure," I tell her. Then with me at the wheel, Grandma gives directions. And after about fifteen minutes, we pull up to the same spot we came to earlier today. Only now, in this dimmer light, the swampy area takes on a different look, kind of creepy with shadowy moss hanging from trees and the haunting sounds of birds and frogs. I really feel like I'm in a foreign country. Maybe Africa.

"Park over there." She points to a small clearing about thirty feet from the edge of the greenish-looking water.

"Be quiet," she says in a low voice as I put on the brake. Then she points out to what looks like a partially submerged log, and I realize it's moving—and that it's actually an alligator. Then I notice there's another one halfway onto the shore, making its way to the chicken scraps Grandma tossed out today.

"That's Bill and Gloria," she whispers.

"How can you tell?"

"You get to know these things after a while."

And so we sit there just watching in silence as these two munch down and fight for the chicken scraps. And although I know it's wrong and it's breaking the law, I have to admit that it's kind of exciting.

"We better go before it starts getting dark," Grandma finally says.

So I head back toward her house. "Do you worry about getting in trouble with the law?" I ask her after we're a ways from the swamp.

She tosses back her head and laughs. "I've never seen any authorities around here, Kimmy. I doubt that anyone even knows about this place 'sides Garth and me. It was Sid who got us coming here in the first place. I suppose if there were folks living round these parts, well, then I'd surely stop feeding my gators. As it is, I can't see that it does any harm. Just don't tell anyone, Kimmy. I'm too old to go to prison." Then she laughs again.

And there it is—my grandmother turns out to be even more of a character than I imagined. Besides illegally feeding the alligators, she was once an unwed mother. Who knew? And oh yeah, she enjoys smoking a pipe occasionally. That took me by surprise the first time I saw her light up.

"It's Sid's old pipe," she told me as she leaned back in the rocker on the porch. "Sometimes I miss the smell. I don't really inhale the smoke though, my old lungs can't take it. But I do enjoy the aroma of a good pipe."

Tonight before I go to bed, I dig through my big manila envelope of hard-copy letters to see if I can find one of the ones that had to do with being pregnant. I remember skimming over a couple recently. Of course, I set them aside because I was so stressed out by Natalie's problems at the time. But tonight I feel like dealing with one.

Dear Jamie,

I am sixteen and pregnant and have decided to keep my baby. He's due in early September, which means I should be able to go back to school after he's born (while he's in day care). But my boyfriend, who's eighteen, doesn't like the idea of having our baby in day care. He thinks we should get married and I should stay home and take care of the baby and just get my GED. I think I'm too young to get married. And I'm not even sure that I want to quit school yet. What do you think I should do?

Teen Mom

Dear Teen Mom,

It sounds like you've given this some thought since you seem certain you're going to parent your baby. As a teenager myself, I can't imagine how hard that would be, but I'm sure you must have some idea. If not, hopefully you will look into it before you make your final decision, because I firmly believe that adoption is a great option. But regarding your question about marriage and high school...it sounds like you know what you want because you have already stated that: 1) you're not ready to get married, and 2) you're not ready to quit high school. So when in doubt, don't. Good luck.

Just Jamie

Sixteen

Sunday, June 30

I can't believe I've been down in Florida for more than two weeks now. I'll admit that the first week was the hardest, and looking back I think I was actually a little depressed. I guess it was similar to culture shock. Like not only had I gone to a totally different part of the country, but it also seemed as if I'd gone back in time as well. Just the idea of being so disconnected from everyone back home was pretty unsettling. But once I survived the first week, it's like I fell into a routine of sorts. And as it turned out, it's a very comfortable routine. I'm just not sure how much longer it needs to continue.

For the first few days, I felt compelled to go to town every day. I'd get in the old Jeep pickup and rattle down the road until my brain felt like mush just so I could check my e-mail and see what was going on in the "real" world. But then I started slacking off—it's like I realized the "real" world would go on without me just fine.

After several days, Uncle Garth finished his woodworking project and began to introduce me to the various things to see down here. He has a "lady friend" named Anna Lee who comes along. But as far as I can tell, they're not romantically involved—just really good friends. So far we've been to several animal refuges, where I've seen some amazing birds and things and gotten some incredible photos. We've also gone fishing a few times—right out on the ocean, which was totally amazing.

And Uncle Garth and Anna Lee showed me the best place to snorkel, and I bought some of those disposable cameras that work underwater. And last week I started taking scuba lessons from the shop that's run by Anna Lee's son, Jacob, and I will become "certified" tomorrow after I take my open water dive test. So it's not like I've had lots of time to sit around and feel sorry for myself.

In the spare time I do have—when I'm not helping Grandma in the kitchen or garden or with any of the other various household chores—I've been getting in a lot of reading. My favorite spot to read is the swing on the screened-in front porch. And Grandma has this great collection of old books. My favorites have been by Gene Stratton-Porter. At first they seemed kind of old-fashioned and quaint, but after I got used to her style, I began to almost imagine that I was living in some of the stories. Especially in "Girl of the Limberlost."

It's also helped me to get over my fear of crawly things. I've actually learned to appreciate the beauty in things like centipedes and salamanders. And Uncle Garth is great at recognizing wildlife. He's given me several books with great photos to study.

I feel like I can just be myself here. And I'm more relaxed than I've been in ages. It's as if I can breathe again. As a result, I have become much less obsessed with some of the stuff that's going on back at home. I still e-mail Dad, Matthew, Natalie, and Maya, but it's not like I'm so immersed in their lives and their problems anymore. And the weird thing is, their lives seem to be getting better—without me. Go figure.

Dad has started going to a therapy group for people who've lost loved ones to cancer. Maya has been in contact with her famous dad, telling him that her mom is having some problems. Matthew is pretty much having a good time touring Europe, and his e-mails have become fewer and shorter—but instead of freaking over this, I'm just realizing that it's okay. And my e-mails to him are similar. Does this mean we're breaking up? I don't think so. But I'm not going to obsess about it. Time will tell.

Unfortunately, Nat just seems to be stuck, like she's in a holding pattern. She still hasn't told her mom or Ben or anyone else—besides the people at Haven, that is. Although she said that all her jeans are too tight now and she's having to wear sweats and is worried someone's going to guess.

There's only one thing that's really bothering me since I've come down here, and that's my relationship with God. It's like it's still going slightly sideways on me. Like I can't quite grasp what it is I'm doing wrong, and I don't know how to fix it. So I've just sort of let it go. Not that I've quit believing in God. That's not it at all. But it's like I've quit trying so hard. And sometimes I feel guilty because I'm not praying as much as I used to pray. And I've only read the Bible a couple of times since I got here. And I haven't gone to any form of fellowship—not even a church service.

Uncle Garth and Grandma don't go to church. But as far as I can tell, based on things they've said, they are both believers. And I've seen my grandma reading her Bible sometimes. I've considered asking them about their faith, but I'm worried that I'll seem intrusive or nosy. It's like their faith is just this quiet thing—it's there, but they don't speak of it much.

The strange thing about all this is that I don't feel extremely worried about it. I get this feeling that God is up to something, that He has me here for a reason, and that everything is going to be fine. I can't even explain how I know this. Maybe it's just a peace that's deep down inside of me.

Tuesday, July 2

I called Dad yesterday afternoon. I just wanted to hear his voice and to tell him that I got certified for scuba diving.

"Congratulations!" he told me. "I'm proud of you, Kim."

"It was so cool, Dad. I wasn't even scared. And it's so great going down under the water. So much quieter than snorkeling. Like a whole different world."

"Sounds great, sweetie."

"I wish you could come to Grandma's," I said suddenly. "Hey, why don't you take some time off, have a little vacation?"

"I'd love to, Kim, but you know that I used up all my vacation time...and then some."

"Yeah," I said, remembering how Dad had taken Mom and me on some special trips before she died.

"Well, maybe you and I can come back here some other time," I told him. "And you can get certified for scuba."

"I've heard of a class here at the community college. They hold it at the pool and then you go to the lake for your final dive."

"Cool."

"Yeah," he said and his voice was enthusiastic, almost happy even. "That would be cool."

So I continued telling him about some of the strange sea creatures I saw today, and he sounded really interested, like he really would like to come down here and try this out, as well as to get reacquainted with Garth and his mom. He almost sounded like my old dad, the one I knew before Mom got sick.

"When do you think you'd like to come home?" he asked in a hesitant tone. We were just getting ready to say good-bye.

"I don't know for sure."

"You've been having such a great time..." He paused. "I wasn't sure if you ever wanted to come back."

"Oh, Dad."

"And I really want you to stay as long as you like, Kim. I think it's been a healthy break for you. And I know Mom and Garth love having you around. The last time I spoke to Mom she was gushing about what a terrific girl you are. Not that I don't agree, of course."

"Actually, I was starting to feel like maybe it was time to come home," I admitted. "But it'll be hard to leave this place. I feel so incredibly comfortable here. It's odd, like I just kind of fit in—and yet it's so totally different than home. Isn't that weird?"

"I don't know, Kim. But I believe the change has been just what you needed. I'm glad you're down there."

"Well, for sure I don't want to come home before the Fourth of July celebration on Thursday. Both Grandma and Uncle Garth say it's something you don't want to miss. But maybe after that..."

"Want me to look into scheduling your return ticket for this weekend?" He sounded hopeful now, and I wondered if he'd been missing me more than he let on.

"Sure, Dad. That sounds great."

So it was settled. He'd get back to me with the details. But after we hung up, I wasn't so sure that I was quite ready to go home yet.

And when I told Grandma and Uncle Garth about this decision, they were clearly disappointed.

"But you just got here," said Grandma.

"And you just got your scuba certificate," said Uncle Garth.

"I know, but I think my dad might be lonely."

"Oh, well," said Grandma quickly. "Then it's understandable."

Uncle Garth nodded. "Yeah, it's not good to be lonely."

Friday, July 5

I can't believe that I'll be leaving here tomorrow morning. Part of me is excited to get home, to see my friends, and get back to my old life again. But another part of me is sad. I feel like I could just stay here forever. Although I suspect that may be a bit of escapist thinking—like I'm scared to go back and face my life. I still remember what Nat said—how lucky I was to be able to run away from my problems. And maybe that's not completely untrue. But then everyone needs to take a break sometimes.

The fireworks display over the bay was absolutely fantastic last night. We fixed a picnic dinner and rode into town in Grandma's Cadillac, getting ourselves a good spot close to the water where we set up lawn chairs. I was surprised at how many people stopped by to say hello. I didn't realize that Grandma had so many friends. And of course, Uncle Garth's friends came by too. But I know most of them by now. They're just regular folks who work here and there in town, leading simple lives, who are pretty laid back and easygoing. It really is a different world, and I think the rest of the world could learn a thing or two from it. Like how to relax and just lighten up.

I felt sad as I packed my things tonight—sorry that this would be the last time (at least for this summer) that I'd get to stay in my little seashell room, listening to the frogs and crickets and all the other wildlife critters that live on the other side of the screened window. But I felt something else too. I wasn't even sure what it was at first, but it's like something was gnawing at me, just beneath my skin. Not literally, of course, that would be creepy. But something was tugging at me, nudging me, nagging at me to pay attention.

Finally, I got everything packed and ready to go. And I was just standing here in this sweet little room, looking around and trying to figure out what was bothering me. What was it?

And then, almost as if I was having a panic attack, my heart started pounding hard. I put my hand on my chest just to see if it was real or something I was imagining. But I could feel it—it's as if I was ready for something to happen—like fight or flight, the adrenaline rush that energizes you to do something. I just didn't know what. So I stood there quietly waiting. Feeling as if the roof was about to cave in. Or an earthquake. Or perhaps an alligator going to bust through my door and take a bite of me.

And then I knew—somehow deep inside me I knew—it was God. It's like He was trying to get my attention. And although I had no idea why this would be happening to me, I knew without doubt that I wanted to listen. And so I actually got on my knees. Right there on the wood plank floor, I knelt down and closed my eyes and I waited.

Now I know this might sound hokey or phony or just plain bizarre, and I'm not even sure that I want to tell anyone about all the details yet, besides writing them in my diary, but I felt as if God reached down in that very moment and just touched me, right on the top of my head. There was this hot feeling, almost like electricity, that ran right through me. And somehow I knew that it really was God, that He was touching me. And somehow I knew, and I totally believe, that He was empowering me. Just like that.

I stayed on my knees for a while, just thanking God and praising Him for whatever it was He was doing, and finally I knew it was time to stand up. So I opened my eyes and looked around, but everything in my room seemed the same as before. Everything in its proper place. The only thing that seemed different was me.

I felt this rush of hope and excitement, like I was on the verge of something powerful and wonderful—a crossroads of sorts. And for the first time since accepting Christ last fall, I felt like I really had God's power running through me, bolstering me up. Did that mean I could do miracles, like moving mountains or making blind men see? Well, I don't know about that. But I felt like whatever kind of power He was giving me, it was going to be life changing. And perhaps even more important, I realized that <u>God would be the One in control</u>. Not me. This wasn't up to me. And that was an enormous relief.

So then I unzipped my carry-on bag and pulled out the Bible I'd already packed. I could remember reading the part where Jesus' disciples had been waiting for Him to reappear after He'd risen from the dead. I knew it was in the New Testament, as I recalled it came directly after the gospels.

I finally found what I was looking for in the first two chapters of Acts. And as I read about the people gathered together, just praying and waiting, I could understand (in a small way) what was happening. And I could relate to how God's power, <u>His Holy Spirit</u>, just swept through that place and how everyone in there was changed—and empowered. It made perfect sense to me. And I believe that God has filled me with His Holy Spirit—in much the same way.

Okay, I haven't discovered any ability to speak in a

foreign language, but I'm open. Mostly I just know that
God is REAL, that He is changing me, and that He's
going to do something amazing in my life. <u>I just know it</u>.
And best of all is that HE'S going to do it. Not me. This
isn't up to me. I just need to be ready, to be listening, to
be available. And I think I can do that. I really do.

Seventeen

Saturday, July 6

I was flying high when the plane took off from Naples
this morning.

"You sure look happy today, Kim," Uncle Garth had
commented as he drove us, speeding again, to the
airport. "You must be glad to be going home."

"That's not it," I told him and Grandma.

"What is it then?" Grandma asked from the backseat.

"Well, I'm sure part of it is because I've had such a
great visit here. But I also feel excited about what God is
doing in my life."

"What's He doing?" Uncle Garth asked as he passed
a farm truck.

"I'm not totally sure," I admitted. "But I just have a
feeling that He's got some really great things ahead for
me."

"I'm sure you're right," said Grandma. "I think God has big plans for you, Kimmy. I'm just so glad that you got to come out here and see us for a spell. And I hope you'll keep in touch. Almost makes me want to get a computer like you use to send that electric mail."

I laughed. "E-mail. Well, don't worry. I can write real letters too. And I promise that I will."

"Good," said Grandma. "I reckon I'm too old to figure out these modern contraptions anyway. And I do love getting letters in the mail."

I hugged them and thanked them at the front door to the airport. "You don't need to come inside. I'll be just fine."

"Such a grown-up young lady," Grandma said as she pinched my cheek. "Can't say I fattened you up any. But your color is good."

"Thanks."

"Get that package from the trunk," Grandma said suddenly. "I almost forgot."

Uncle Garth ran to the back of the car and returned with a bundle wrapped in brown paper and tied with a string.

"What is it?" I asked as I tucked the soft package under my arm.

"The crazy quilt," she told me. "I wanted you to have it—something to remember us by."

Then, waving at them, I took my bags and went inside. And I guess I wasn't surprised to discover that my face was wet. I'd obviously been crying.

I felt amazingly calm and relaxed as I waited in the check-in line and went through security and then finally boarded my plane, which was nearly an hour late in taking off. I knew this might mess me up on my next flight, and yet I wasn't concerned about this. I honestly believe this was due to what God is doing in me. It's like I have this new confidence—a deep peace—like I really believe that God is in control and that I'm going to be okay.

That doesn't mean I think my life is going to be perfect. I don't imagine that I'll be floating on clouds or walking on sunshine. Although I suppose that part of me would like it to be like that. But I have this strong suspicion that will not be the case. And that's okay.

I was running late when I got off my flight to switch planes in Orlando. And when I discovered the gate I needed to get to was quite a ways away, I decided to run. Maybe God had delayed that flight and I was going to make it. But by the time I reached the gate, the plane had already taken off. The woman at the gate rearranged my ticket, which meant I now had a layover of nearly three hours.

Okay, I admit I felt a little dismayed. What was I supposed to do for that long in the Orlando airport? Now if the delay had been really long, like eight hours, I might've been tempted to go to Disney World. I had just gotten a frozen yogurt when I heard someone yelling my name.

I looked across the concourse and saw Allie Curtis

waving frantically from the moving walkway. I couldn't believe it! Was it possible that their rock band, Redemption, was performing around here? I hurried to catch her, jogging alongside the walkway as I tried to keep up.

"What are you doing here?" she asked.

"I'm on my way home. I was visiting my grandma down near Naples. What are you doing here?"

"We just got here. I forgot this," she held up a backpack, "on the plane so I had to run back and get it. The others are waiting for me at Starbucks." The moving walkway ended, and she hopped off and grabbed me by the hand. "Come on down here and say hi, Kim. Have you got time?"

Already we were on the next moving walkway. "Yeah," I told her, catching my breath. "I've got almost three hours to kill."

"Cool."

Before I knew it we were all sitting at Starbucks— Chloe, Allie, and Laura and I. It was so awesome.

"The others went to pick up our bags and the car," Chloe explained. "We've got a concert at the Christian book convention tonight."

"I can't believe I'm seeing you guys," I said, still astonished. "It has to be a God-thing."

So we sat and talked for a few minutes, then Allie and Laura decided to run over to the sunglasses shop since Allie had broken her favorite pair of shades. "We'll be right back," they said.

And then, I'm not quite sure why, I proceeded to tell Chloe about what had happened to me last night. And she just nodded and smiled.

"I know exactly what you mean," she said after I finished. "That is so cool, Kim."

"So, do you think it's what I think? I mean, the part about the Holy Spirit?"

She nodded. "I'm sure it is."

"That's so amazing." I laughed. "And then meeting you guys here. It's like God is so in control."

"But let me warn you about something."

"Yeah?"

"While it's totally cool to feel like that—like you're high as a kite but without using drugs—you need to remember that the feeling won't always be there like that."

"I sort of thought about that. I mean, I've always been such a realist."

Chloe laughed. "You and me both."

"So what happens then?"

"It's just like life—you have your ups and downs, but you know that God is still with you, He's still in control. And that sustains you."

Then Allie and Laura came back, both sporting some pretty cool shades. "They have everything over there," Allie told us. "You should check it out, Kim."

"Well, I've got plenty of time for that."

"Speaking of time," Laura said, looking at her watch. "The limo is probably waiting for us."

So we all hugged. But before they left, Chloe reached into her bag. "Hey, I just read this C. S. Lewis book, Kim. You want it for the trip home?"

"Sure." I reached for the smallish book, thinking I'd probably have it read before my flight even took off.

"It's a lot heavier than it looks," Chloe said. "But I think you'll get it."

And so I went back to my gate and started reading "The Screwtape Letters." And it is totally unlike anything I've ever read before. But Chloe was right on. I am definitely getting it. And I'm trying to read it slowly so I can take it all in. Amazing stuff. Already, I can tell that I'm going to be a C. S. Lewis fan.

I take a reading break to check my e-mail. I haven't been online since the Fourth of July celebration, and then only briefly. It looks like Matthew and his grandpa are getting tired of traveling. Matthew says they'll be home by July 20 and that he can't wait to see me. And normally I would think this was great news, but for some reason, I'm not so sure now. Still, I can think about that later.

There's also a sweet note from Dad wishing me "happy travels" and warning me that a few things have changed around the house. This has me pretty curious. I e-mail back, telling him about my delayed flight and that I'll call him later on my cell phone, in case he's not checking e-mail today.

The e-mail from Maya is hard to decipher. She sounds like she's really mad at her mom, but that she's

also working on some kind of mysterious plan. My
guess is she's going to go live with her dad. Although
with her dad on tour, I'm not sure how that will work.
Even so, I write back and encourage her to get on with
her life—and not to let her mom's bad choices drag her
down. I also remind her that I'm still praying for her and
that I think the only way she'll ever get the direction she
really needs is to come to God. He's the One with the
answers.

The last e-mail is from Natalie. I had e-mailed her on
Thursday to let her know I'd be home this weekend.
And while she seems relieved, she also still sounds
bitter, like I'm somehow to blame for her troubles. But
instead of getting irritated, I just pray for her. And in my
response I tell her that no matter what she does about
this pregnancy, her life will never get better without
God—period. Then I hit send.

I don't get home until nearly seven o'clock—four
hours later than expected. Oh, well. But Dad is waiting
for me down in baggage claim. He has flowers and a
"Welcome Home" balloon, and I burst into tears when I
see him. We hug for a long time, and it occurs to me
how much I love him and how much I need him. And
I'm thinking maybe he feels the same way.

"Now, I warned you about some changes at home,"
he tells me as he drives away from the airport. "I hope
you won't mind."

"What kind of changes?"

"Well, I've been going to that therapy group...and

one of the steps toward recovering from this is to take control. For me that meant I should remove some of the things that made me sad. I know it might sound silly, but every time I walked past the couch in the family room, I would look at it and remember your mother sitting there, feeling bad because of the cancer, and that memory would blot out the happier ones."

"Yeah?"

"So I got rid of the couch."

"Oh." I'm not sure how to respond as I suddenly imagine our entire house stripped of furniture.

"Do you mind?"

I consider this. "No, I think I know what you mean. I probably have had some of those same feelings about that couch."

"And naturally, I don't want to change everything, Kim. There are lots of things I like because they remind me of your mother and the happier times. I just needed to feel as if I had some control now. Do you understand?"

"I think I do."

We stop to eat a late dinner on the way home. And to my surprise, Dad continues to talk about Mom and what he's doing to get through the grieving process.

"I realize you can't rush these things. But it does no good to put them off either. There is a way to recover, and I'm working toward that."

"I'm so glad for you, Dad."

"I went through her personal things last week, Kim.

I'm keeping the items that have meaning for me, and I thought maybe you'd want to go through them too. And then we can donate what's left to the Salvation Army."

I nod. "Yeah, that's probably good." Still, the idea of going through Mom's personal stuff is a little unsettling. It makes everything seem so final. Not that it isn't final, but I guess I've been putting it off too.

Anyway, I try not to act too surprised when I get home and see that some things are gone. I'm not even sure why it was that Dad got rid of certain things and kept others. But I guess I'm okay with it. And after I get over the shock of seeing some bare spots, I think Dad is right. It's like we really do need a new beginning.

"I know you're probably worn out from traveling," Dad says after I have a chance to look around. "But maybe you'd like to go furniture shopping with me tomorrow. I'm sure I could use some help."

"Sure," I tell him. "Is after church okay?"

He nods. "And I've gone back to church too, Kim. You were right; I needed that more than I realized."

"Good for you, Dad."

"And I feel close to your mom when I'm there. I think it makes her happy too."

"I'm sure it does." I consider telling Dad about my own incredible spiritual experience last night, but I'm just not sure if it's the right time. I don't want to overwhelm him. I'd also like to talk to him about the situation with his birth dad too, but I think that will be a timing thing as well. In the meantime, I think it's okay to just wait.

"It's good to have you home, sweetie." He gives me another hug.

And even though I miss some things about Grandma's house, I'm really glad to be home too. It feels pretty good to put my things in my room. I arrange some of the pretty shells I found on my dresser and bedside table, and I stick some of my better photos on my bulletin board. I plan to have some of them enlarged and framed later on down the line. And then when I finally put Grandma's crazy quilt on my bed, it feels just like home.

I consider calling Natalie but decide it can wait. It feels later than it actually is, but it's probably because I'm still on Florida time. Finally, I answer some letters before I fall asleep.

Dear Jamie,

My dad died when I was three, and it was just Mom and me for the next ten years. Then "John" came into the picture. They dated for a while, then Mom married him last year. The problem is, he thinks he's the boss of me now. And he makes all these rules that I think are totally stupid. It's like all he wants to do is get me into trouble so he can yell at me. I hate being yelled at. And I hate being grounded (like I am right now). Sometimes I want to kill this man. Or maybe I should just run away. What should I do?

Desperate Daughter

Dear DD,

    I'm sure that must be very hard for you. And neither of your options (killing him or running away) will solve your problems. I suggest you talk to your mom. Tell her how you are feeling. Ask her if there's some way she can step in and straighten this guy out. The way I see it, she's your mom and she should be the one who deals with you. If this doesn't work, maybe you should ask your mom and stepdad to join you in meeting with a good family counselor. Good luck.

    Just Jamie

Eighteen

Thursday, July 11

It felt like Natalie and I were having a standoff again. She assumed that since I came home, I would be willing to take her in to get an abortion. And when I told her I couldn't do that, she got mad. But instead of getting mad back at her, I told her that I wanted to be supportive of her, I wanted to help her through this pregnancy, and that I would be her friend no matter what. Of course, this only seemed to make her angrier.

"So you're saying that you're okay hanging with me when my belly is sticking out to here." She held her arms in a wide circle for a visual aid.

"Yeah," I told her.

"You're not the least bit embarrassed to go to the mall, youth group, school, whatever...with a big, fat pregnant best friend?"

I considered this. To be honest, I might feel somewhat embarrassed. "Okay, I might be a little uncomfortable at first. But after I got used to—"

"Well, don't worry," she snapped. "You won't need to get used to it, Kim. I'm not having this baby."

"How far along are you now?"

"Three months." She leaned back on the new leather sofa that Dad and I picked out on Sunday and folded her arms across her chest (which has become bigger since I've been gone).

"And you still won't tell anyone?"

She just glared at me.

"Not even a counselor?"

More glaring.

"Well." I stood up now. "I think this is wrong."

"What?"

"You keeping this to yourself. I think Ben has a right to know, and I think your mom has a right to know."

"It's my body."

"But it's Ben's baby. And you are your mother's daughter. And what if you get an abortion and something goes wrong, and there are complications? You think your mom won't find out then? And how's that going to make her feel?"

"Look." Nat stood too. "If all you're going to do is lecture me, I can just split. You made me think that you were going to help me when you came home. But all you do is make me feel worse. I don't need this kind of crud from you, Kim."

"I'm sorry," I said in a calm voice. "But I think you do need this. You're not thinking clearly, Nat. It's like being pregnant has depleted your brain cells."

"Thanks."

"I just want to discuss this with you. And it's like all you want to do is fight, Nat. I don't want to fight. I just want to help you."

"If you want to help me, you can take me to Haven next Tuesday. I've rescheduled for ten that morning."

"I can't help you do something I think will hurt you," I said, and not for the first time.

"It's not your decision, Kim."

"It's my decision whether I help you or not. And I will not help you to get an abortion."

She was heading for the door now. But I got in front of her.

"And the reason I won't help you is because I know that you'd be even more miserable afterward than you were before."

"You know?" She narrowed her eyes at me. "How can you possibly know how I feel, Kim? Or how I'd feel afterward?"

"Because I love you, Nat. And I've been praying for you. And I just know this in the same way that I know how bad you need God in your life right now. I just know."

"Yeah, right." Then she pushed past me and left, slamming the door behind her.

Saturday, July 13

I went to youth group tonight. And it was so cool to be there. So great to hang with people who believe like I do. It was REAL fellowship. And I got to wondering, had everyone here changed? Or was it just me?

When it was time to share about what God's been doing in our lives, I actually raised my hand. It's like I couldn't NOT raise my hand.

Cesar, who was leading the group tonight since Josh and Caitlin are still down in Mexico (following their honeymoon), smiled and pointed at me. "Yeah, Kim, what's up? We've been really missing you around here."

So I stood and told them about what had happened to me just a week ago, how I got down on my knees in the bedroom at Grandma's house and everything. I even mentioned how I ran into the Redemption girls in Orlando and how Chloe really confirmed to me that it was a God-thing. Not that I'd had any doubts.

"That's awesome," Cesar said and everyone clapped, which actually made me feel rather silly, like I was a trained seal or something. But I'm sure that's not how they meant it to come across. They were just happy for me.

After that some of the others, not everyone, shared how they'd had similar spiritual experiences. But all the stories were different. We finally agreed that God works in a variety of unexplainable and creative ways.

Afterward as we were pigging out on junk food, Ben came over to talk to me. I tried to smile and act natural, but it was really hard not to think about Natalie as he talked.

"That is so great to hear, Kim." He slapped me on the back. "Very cool."

"Thanks," I managed to mutter, glancing over my shoulder for someone else to interrupt us.

"Uh, I've been meaning to ask, but you were gone…" Ben glanced around too, as if he was uncomfortable. "Anyway, how is Natalie doing? I never see her around, and well, I guess I'm worried about her." His face got really sad. "And I guess I've really been struggling with guilt about everything, you know?"

I nodded without speaking.

"And I, uh, usually talk to Josh about stuff like this, but he's been gone and stuff. So I'm not really sure what to do." He looked at me with the most helpless expression.

"I, uh, I don't know what to tell you, Ben."

"Have you talked to her much? Is she doing okay?"

And then it's like something in me just broke. I'd like to think it was a God-thing, but I'm not totally sure.

"Okay, Ben, I want to tell you something, but it needs to be private. Can we go in the sanctuary or something?"

He looked around at our friends as they joked and ate, then nodded. Thankfully, he hadn't brought Torrey with him tonight. That would've complicated things.

We headed for the sanctuary but discovered Willy was there setting up some things for the worship time tomorrow, so we decided to go out to the parking lot.

Finally, when I was sure no one could overhear us, I shot up a silent prayer and then told Ben to brace himself.

"Natalie is pregnant," I said slowly and clearly, "with your child, Ben."

Even in the dimly lit parking lot, I could see the color draining from his face. He almost looked like he was going to fall over.

I put my hand on his shoulder. "Are you okay?"

He just shook his head.

"I'm sorry. I hate that you have to learn about it like this. I've begged Nat to tell you, but she refuses. I'm the only one, well, other than Haven—"

"Haven?" His eyes got wide.

I nodded. "Yeah, she wants to get an abortion."

Ben pushed his hand through his short-cropped blond hair and let out a big groan. "Oh, man."

"I don't know what to do, Ben. I know that an abortion would kill Nat. I don't mean physically, but inside. She's always been so against it. And just losing her virginity has nearly destroyed her. I've tried talking her out of it, but she won't listen. She refuses to get counseling and—"

"I can't take this," he said as he fiercely shook his head. "I'm sorry, but I just can't handle it. I gotta get out of here, Kim." Then he took off running.

Just as he left, Cesar came up. "Something wrong?" he asked with genuine concern in his voice.

By then I was crying. "Oh, Cesar, I don't know what to do. I hope I haven't made a mistake."

"Want to talk?"

So, feeling miserable and confused, I spilled the whole story to Cesar. I honestly didn't know what else to do. "You can't tell anyone." I made him promise after I was done. "I'm serious, Nat would probably kill me...or herself."

"Don't worry, your secret is safe. But I want to talk to Ben. I'm thinking he probably needs a friend right now."

Well, there was some comfort in that. And of all the guys in the youth group, I felt certain that Cesar would be the most mature and understanding. But I didn't want to go back in for the fellowship time. I just couldn't. So I got in my Jeep and drove home. But as I drove, I prayed. I prayed for Ben and Cesar. And for Nat. And the amazing thing was that my prayer felt very real and powerful. As if God Himself was helping me to pray. That was some consolation.

Sunday, July 14

I went to church and looked all over for Ben, but I never saw him. I did talk to Cesar, and he said he'd called Ben and left a message. "But I haven't heard back from him yet."

"I hope he's okay." I shook my head sadly. "He was so upset. This is such a mess."

"Yeah. Not exactly what God had in mind, is it?"

"You got that right."

On my way home, I was wondering about Natalie. Was it possible that Ben would contact her now? That she would find out I was the one who spilled the beans? And would it be better to confess this now, or risk her wrath later? I wasn't sure. But I knew who to ask.

And I had barely said "amen" when I knew that I needed to come clean with Natalie. And even though I knew this for a fact, I couldn't think of anything I'd rather NOT do. In fact, I even started making up excuses why this would be a bad day to do this. I reminded myself of the "patient" in "The Screwtape Letters," being influenced by Wormwood's lies.

So without even going in my house first, I parked my Jeep in the driveway and marched over to Natalie's house, bracing myself, I'm sure, for the spitfire word-bashing beating I was about to receive.

"What's up?" Nat asked when she opened the door looking like she just woke up.

"Is your mom back from church?"

"Not yet."

Knowing that Nat's family could be back soon, I decided that maybe we should take this someplace else. "Get something on your feet," I commanded her. "We're going for a walk."

To my surprise, she didn't argue as she slipped on her flip-flops and joined me outside. "What's up, Kim?"

"We need to talk."

She rolled her eyes. "Another lecture?"

"Not exactly."

We got about a block from our street, and I took a deep breath. "I have a confession."

She turned and looked at me, then almost laughed. "I know what it is—you lost your virginity too? I'll bet it happened in Florida, huh? Tell me about it."

"No," I said, trying to conceal my disgust that she'd jump to this conclusion. "That's not it."

"Well, what then?"

"I was at youth group last night. And afterward, Ben came up to talk to me. He was really concerned about you, Nat. He wanted to know how you were doing, and well, I'm not sure what came over me—maybe it was God, but—"

She stopped walking and grabbed me by the shoulders. "You didn't?" Her eyes looked like hot blue heat. "You didn't tell him, did you?"

"It's like I couldn't help it, Nat."

"No!" she screamed. "Kim, I trusted you."

"But he deserved to know…he's part of this, Nat. He's the father—"

Then Nat used some profanity I'd never heard her use. And I was so shocked that I couldn't even say anything. And she turned away from me and walked off. I couldn't even call after her. I just stood there.

And I guess I am second-guessing myself now. Like was I wrong to tell Ben? Have I really betrayed my best friend? What should I have done instead? Finally as a distraction, I decide to Just Ask Jamie again.

Dear Jamie,

I made a promise to my best friend. And then I broke it. But the reason I broke it was because I thought it was really in her best interest. I thought that keeping my promise would only allow her to really hurt herself—in a way that she might never recover from. But now she hates me, and I'm sure she'll never speak to me again. I feel horrible. What should I do?

Promise Breaker

Dear PB,

Not knowing the nature of your promise, it's hard to know what to tell you. But if you really did believe your friend was going to harm herself—like if she was considering suicide or breaking the law or something that she would really regret—perhaps it was better to break your promise. Of course, now that you've lost her trust, it's possible that you've lost her friendship too. I suggest that you apologize for breaking your promise and try to explain your reasoning. If she refuses to listen, you'll probably just have to wait and see if she comes to her senses. Hopefully whatever you did (that broke your promise) will cause something in her situation to change for the better, and she'll see why you did it.

Just Jamie

Okay, I know this sounds crazy, but I'm thinking, hey, why didn't I think of that? And then I realize that I did—sort of. And I think that's probably true. I may just have to step aside and wait and see what happens next. But I'll be praying. I will most definitely be praying! Not only that, but I think I'll run this letter in the column. It's not like it really gives anything away. And maybe Nat will read it.

Nineteen

Tuesday, July 16

I didn't hear anything back from Natalie for a couple of days. Although I did e-mail her an apology and an explanation. It was nothing I hadn't already said before—lots of times—but I figured I probably owed her as much.

But at about nine-thirty this morning, I go out to the porch and sit in the shadows to keep watch on Natalie's house. Naturally, I am worried that she'll get into the Toyota pickup and head off, I would assume, to Haven. And as much as I would like to follow her there, and somehow derail her, I have this strong feeling that I am NOT supposed to do that. So I just sit on the porch, praying—for a miracle.

It's about a quarter to ten when I see Ben's car pull into her driveway. And I nearly jump out of my chair to run over there and ask him what on earth he thinks he's doing. Why is he showing up at Nat's at the same time she's scheduled an abortion? Is it possible that he supports Natalie in her decision to go through with this? Why haven't I even considered this possibility? Why did I even trust him in the first place? I want to scream.

Of course, I'm telling myself now, why would Ben want everyone (including his girlfriend and brother-in-law youth pastor) to know that he's the father of Natalie's baby? Why haven't I thought of this?

So, feeling sick to my stomach, I sit and watch as Ben goes to the front door and returns with Natalie, walking her to his car. He even opens the door for her. Then they drive away. Just like that. No big deal. They could just as easily be going for a picnic as to have their unborn child murdered.

Okay, at this point, I am seriously considering following them and somehow making this craziness stop right here, right now. But how? Besides, I still have this very strong feeling (I think it's God) that that would be wrong. So I just sit here and pray—and pray and pray.

And I must say that praying makes a difference. Despite how worried I am for Nat and her unborn baby, and despite how angry I feel at Ben for this, I still have this deep sense of peace. I am trusting that somehow God will bring good out of what appears to be nothing but crud.

Even so, it's a very long day, and it isn't until this evening that I hear the rest of the story. Even now I'm still pinching myself. It starts with a phone call.

"Hey, Kim," Nat says to me, as if everything between us is just fine.

"Nat?" I'm not quite sure it's really her.

"Yeah, I just wanted to let you know that I didn't do it."

"Didn't do it?"

"I didn't get the abortion."

"Really?" Okay, I want to jump and shout hallelujah now, but I try to contain myself.

"Really."

"What happened?"

"Ben called me on Monday. He said that you'd told him about, well, you know. And he wanted to know what he could do to help."

"Yeah?"

"So, I was still pretty mad at him, and I said the only thing he could do to help would be to take me to Haven for my appointment."

"And he agreed to do that?"

"Yeah. I was kind of surprised too."

I don't admit that I witnessed this little spectacle. "And then what?"

"We got to Haven, the back parking lot, and then Ben just totally broke down. I mean, he was crying and sobbing and apologizing and everything. It was actually pretty sweet."

"And?"

"Well, I started to cry too. And I told him that I didn't

really believe in abortion and that I knew it was wrong and that it made me sick to think I was willing to kill this baby just so that I'd look good."

"Yeah?"

"And he said he felt the same way. He admitted that part of him wanted to sweep it away and pretend like it never happened, and that he thought an abortion would do that."

"And?"

"But that he knew it was wrong. He knew that God didn't want us to destroy this baby."

I take in a big breath and then slowly exhale.

"And you're not going to believe this, Kim." Her voice actually sounds very happy now. And I'm thinking, you're right, I'm not going to believe this.

"But Ben wants to do the right thing. He asked me to marry him, Kim. Can you believe it? We're going to get married! And I want you as my maid of honor. I'm just so happy. And it's all because of you!"

Okay, now I feel sick or like someone just jerked the floor out from under me, and I can't even respond.

"Did you hear me?"

"Yeah," I manage to say. "I guess I'm just shocked, Nat. I mean, this is so sudden."

"Aren't you happy for me?"

I take in another breath. I really do NOT want to blow this. Besides, I am happy for the sake of the baby and Nat's mental health. "Yes, I AM happy for you, Nat. This is incredible."

"And so you'll be my maid of honor?"

"Uh, yeah, of course. I'm just so stunned. It's a lot to process, you know."

"I know. I still think I dreamed the whole thing."

I want to ask her if she's absolutely sure that she didn't. Is it possible she really had the abortion and is just hallucinating from the painkiller? We talk a little bit more, and I try to sound enthused, but all I can think is this is a big mistake. For one thing, Ben doesn't love her. For another thing, they are both like seventeen. How do you start a marriage when you're not even out of high school yet?

Friday, July 19

Nat has not only returned to her old self, but she's also returned to God. And while I know I should be EXTREMELY happy for this—elated and ecstatic—I mostly feel just plain confused. Of course, I don't let on to her. I try to act like I'm with her, like I think the idea of her and Ben getting married during their senior year of high school is a brilliant plan. But all I can think is that it's totally crazy. It reminds me of some of the letters I get for the column.

Natalie finally told her mom. Actually, she and Ben told her mom together. And I have to give it to Ben— that was a pretty honorable thing for him to do. I seriously doubt that Nat could've done it on her own. And as hurt and angry as Mrs. McCabe was—and Nat said she definitely was—she did choose to forgive them. Well, as long as they agreed to go in and see her friend Marge for marriage counseling, and then get married ASAP.

After that, and Natalie said this was the hardest part, they went to Ben's parents and informed them.

"Oh, man, Kim," she told me yesterday. "You should've seen their faces. I honestly thought they were going to blow sky high."

"Did they?"

"Not exactly. His mom got real quiet, and Mr. O'Conner excused himself for a while. It was pretty awful. Then everyone started crying, and Ben told them how sorry he was and how he wished he could've been more like Caitlin. It was really pretty sad."

"I can imagine."

"But I think they're okay," she said brightly.

"Okay?"

"Well, they weren't too sure about us getting married. They made that perfectly clear. And to be honest, I was a little offended. It's like I'm not good enough for—"

"Oh, I doubt it's that. I'm sure they're just worried about how young you guys are and—"

"Well, we're old enough to have a baby," she said. "I guess we're old enough to get married. My mom wasn't much older than me when she got married."

I don't remind her it was a marriage that failed.

"Anyway," she continued happily, "Ben really stood up for me. He insisted it was the right thing to do, and

he said it was his decision and he hoped that they'd
support him on it."

"And will they?"

She shrugged. "I think they'll come around...in time."

For now, I realize I have to keep my thoughts and
opinions to myself about this. I know it wouldn't do any
good for me to rain on Natalie's parade. And crud, she's
been through so much already, why would I want to
spoil this?

Since Natalie's story is quickly becoming "old news,"
I realize it's time to tell my dad. And he's understandably
stunned when I tell him.

"That's the friend who is pregnant?" He looks
incredulous. "But what about her religious convictions?
What about her abstinence pledge?"

I just shake my head. "Promises get broken
sometimes, Dad."

"Poor Mrs. McCabe," he says in a typical parental
reaction. "This must be hard on her."

"Yeah. It is." I don't remind him that it's been pretty
hard on me too.

"So what's our Nat going to do?" He rubs his chin
and frowns.

So I tell him about the almost-abortion. He doesn't
seem surprised, but then he's a newspaper man; he's
heard it all.

Then he reaches over and pats me on the back. "No
wonder you were having such a hard time, Kimmy. That
must've been a heavy load to carry. It makes me even

more glad that I shipped you off to Grandma's."

"Grandma was a real comfort," I tell him, wondering if this is the time to share her story.

"So if Natalie's decided to have the baby, does that mean she plans to keep it, or will she consider giving it up for adoption?"

And so I tell him about the marriage idea.

"You're kidding?"

"Nope. It sounds completely crazy to me, Dad. But they seem totally serious about it."

"I'm glad it sounds crazy to you, Kim. That's a great comfort to a father's weary heart."

"But Natalie seems certain that it's going to happen," I continue. "They've already told their parents."

"And their parents agree?"

"Mrs. McCabe does. I'm not sure about Ben's parents."

Now Dad hugs me. "I'm just glad I'm not in their shoes, Kim. And when I remember how I thought that pregnancy test kit was yours." He lets go of me and just shakes his head. "Well, I'm so sorry, sweetie."

"It was understandable, Dad." I'm still thinking about his mother's story and trying to decide if now is the time. But the phone rings and it turns out to be Matthew.

"Hey, Kim, I'm back in the country!" he says happily.

"Welcome home!"

"Well, not actually home yet. We're in New York for the night. We're going to see a Broadway show tonight."

"Cool."

"I can't wait to see you, babe."

"Yeah," I try to echo his enthusiasm.

"Our flight gets in at five tomorrow. I thought maybe you'd like to go out with me later. I can tell you all about it."

"Sounds great," I tell him.

But when I hang up, I'm not so sure. It feels like something in me has changed in regard to Matthew. I mean, I still care about him, but I'm just not sure....

Dear Jamie,

How do you know if it's the Real Thing? I mean, being in love. I've been going with the same guy for a year, and I can tell he's really into me. He gets me gifts and treats me really great. But sometimes I think I could live without him. So how can he be the one if I think I could live without him?

Fickle

Dear Fickle,

I think you've answered your own question. If you think you could live without this guy, then he's probably NOT the one. But you shouldn't feel too bad. Maybe he is one of the ones who will help you to realize the difference when you actually meet the Real One.

Just Jamie

Twenty

Wednesday, July 24

I broke up with Matthew last weekend. I'm still kind of in shock that I actually did it. But I believe it was the right thing to do. I didn't break up on the first night he came home. That would've been mean.

"Why?" he asked me on Sunday night, after I gently broke the news. "Did you find someone else? Some hunk sweep you off your feet down in Florida?" I could tell by his tone that he felt bad.

I attempted a laugh. "No, not at all. That's crazy. To be totally honest, it's a God-thing, Matthew."

"Meaning that God thinks I'm not good enough for you?"

"No, that's not it, Matthew. I just got a very strong sense that God doesn't want me to date right now."

"Not anyone? Never?"

"Not right now. I'm not sure what comes later on. But for now, I don't think God wants me to date anyone."

"Man!" He actually smacked his fist into the steering wheel of his truck. "And to think of what I gave up in Copenhagen."

"Copenhagen?"

He rolled his eyes. "I met this girl...Anna. We hung together for a couple of days, and she was pretty cool."

"Oh."

"And she was into me."

"Well, maybe you can write to her," I said meekly, fighting an unexpected wave of jealousy.

"I didn't get her address." He shook his head sadly.

Okay, I was feeling a little irked. I mean, here I was breaking up with him, and he was obsessing over this girl he met in Europe. What was up with that? "I can't believe you. You're mad at me because you missed some big opportunity with Anna?"

"That's not what gets me. I just can't believe I was over there being faithful to you when I could've had—" He stopped himself.

"Go ahead. When you could've had <u>what</u>, Matthew?"

He let loose with a foul word, one he knows I find offensive. "You know what I mean, Kim. This girl was really into me—we could've had some fun. But I thought, 'No way, I have a girlfriend back home. I'm going to be faithful to her.' And this is what it gets me."

I was glad that his pickup was parked in front of my

house, because I was about ready to jump out and run inside. Instead, I prayed that God would give me the right words.

"I'm sorry, Matthew," I told him in an even tone. "I honestly didn't see this coming. And it's not even that easy for me. You've been a really good friend to me. A great boyfriend. And it's not your fault—"

"Of course it's not my fault. I didn't do anything to mess this up."

I nodded. "Yeah, I know. And I really am sorry. I hope that you can forgive me—"

"That's for you <u>Christians</u> to do," he snapped. "Us heathens, well, we can just be mad if we want."

"I hate seeing us ending like this," I said as I reached for the door handle.

"Yeah, me too." He turned and looked away.

So I told him good-bye and got out of the truck and walked toward my house. I almost expected him to jump out and say that he was sorry, that he understood what I was going through, that he was really okay with this, and maybe we could still be friends. But he just started his engine, then gunned it and took off with tires squealing down the street. And I started to cry.

I went straight to my room, surprised that I was feeling so bad about this. I mean, it was my decision to break up, wasn't it? Why was I the one crying?

But I know why now. It's because I've hurt Matthew, and that feels horrible. He's been so good to me. Oh, sure, he wasn't perfect. But he never did anything to hurt me. And I hurt him. And that makes me feel sick.

Does that mean I should get back together with him? I carefully consider this. Have I made a mistake?

But deep down inside, I know God wanted me to do this. And I know I have been obedient. And just because it doesn't feel good doesn't mean it was wrong. I just wish it didn't have to hurt so much.

Thursday, August 1

Everyone pretty much knows about Ben and Natalie now. There's been a real mix of reactions. Of course, some were totally shocked. Like Torrey, for instance. I heard, via Natalie, that she threw a complete hissy fit and then left town to go stay with her aunt in California for the rest of summer break. Can't say that I blame her. I mean, if it hurt that much just breaking up with Matthew (when it was my choice), how much more would it hurt to find out that your boyfriend had gotten another girl pregnant? I'm praying for Torrey.

Our youth group was amazingly understanding when the word leaked out. I think Cesar was instrumental in this. Even so, Ben hasn't been back yet. I think it's hard for him still.

Josh and Caitlin will return from Mexico next week. According to Pastor Tony's announcement at midweek service last night, they believe that God has called them to be missionaries in their hometown for the time being. Josh will return to his position as youth pastor, and

Caitlin will assist him and also oversee the children's ministry. I'm not sure if their decision has anything to do with Ben, but I suspect it might've played into things. Anyway, I, for one, will be glad to have them back. They just seem so grounded—and I think we could use that.

Matthew hasn't called me once since the breakup, and I haven't run into him anywhere in town. And I have to admit, there have been times when I've really questioned myself. Like did I really hear God on this? And if so, why am I feeling so miserable now? Because I really do miss Matthew—a lot!

I keep having these flashbacks, recalling all the fun times we had together. And there are moments when I don't really understand why I needed to break it off. But then I remember that it was God's leading, and I do have peace about that. But it's a peace that's wrapped in pain. And I don't completely get that.

I will be so glad when Caitlin is back. I really want to talk to her. I think she'll understand what I'm going through.

Lately, it feels as if I have too much time on my hands. Sort of like the girl who wrote this letter, although I don't think I'd be tempted to do what she's been doing.

Dear Jamie,

I started playing online poker this summer. Mostly because I was bored, and it was something to do. But now it's like I want to do it all the time. And lately, I started to play for money. So far, I've only lost about a

hundred dollars. But I think I could win it back if I try.
I told my best friend about this, and she says I'm
addicted. But I think I'm just having fun. You seem pretty
sensible. Do you think it's wrong to play online poker?
 Poker Joker

Dear Poker Joker,

*First of all, I think it's illegal for minors to gamble
online or otherwise. And you say yourself that you
"want to do it all the time." That sounds pretty addicted
to me. But here's a good way to find out. See if you can
go two weeks without playing. And then if you decide to
play again (just for fun), make sure that no money is
involved and you limit your time. If you can't do that,
then it's time to cash in your chips and find another
form of entertainment.*

Just Jamie

Monday, August 5

I started working at the newspaper office this week. I'm
filling in for the receptionist for two weeks while she
takes her vacation time. My dad thought it was a good
idea, and I have to agree with him. A cool thing
happened today, something that made me realize that
God might be using my column.

"Is my dad in?" asked a familiar-looking girl. Then I
recognized the long, curly auburn hair and remembered.

"Casey?"

She smiled. "Do I know you?"

"I'm Kim. Allen Peterson's daughter."

"Oh, yeah." She smiled. "It's been a while, huh? I thought you were like the new receptionist or something."

"I'm just filling in while Gail's on vacation. And your dad's not here right now. He went to a meeting at city hall. His secretary probably knows when he'll be back."

She nodded but just stood there, as if trying to decide what to do.

"So, how are you doing?" I asked, looking directly into her eyes. I'd totally forgotten all about that last letter she penned to Just Jamie a few months ago. She had sounded so depressed at the time that I'd been worried. But then my life got too crazy, and I just lost track.

"Okay."

"So, what have you been up to this summer?" I continued, curious as to how she was really doing. "Planning any great vacations?"

"Actually, I just got back from this really cool camp." And then she proceeded to tell me about this Young Life camp that sounded amazing.

"Wow, I think I'd like to go there."

Her eyes got big. "You would probably like it, Kim. I mean, it was really fun and everything, but it wasn't just all the stuff they had to do… I mean, it's like a life-changing thing too."

"Cool." Now, even though we don't have Young Life at my school, I know that it's a Christian organization, so

I'm wondering if that's what she's talking about. "Maybe I should mention it to our youth group leader. Maybe we can go there sometime."

She looked at me closely. "Are you a Christian?"

I nodded and smiled.

"Cool!"

"Yeah," I said. "Very cool."

"I am too. I mean, I made a commitment. It's only been a couple of weeks. But I can tell that I'm really changing. I'm lots happier and stuff."

"That's great, Casey. I'm so happy for you."

Then her dad walked in the front door. So we said good-bye and promised to talk more later. And I just about did a happy dance in my chair because I was so thankful that God had gotten a hold of Casey Snow! And then I remembered how she'd been on my prayer list for a while last spring. Back before my little meltdown when I quit praying and got shipped off to Grandma's to recover. But it made me think that God really was listening to me—even when it didn't really feel like it.

Thursday, August 15

Natalie and I met for lunch today. She brought along some wedding magazines to look at, and I tried to feign enthusiasm, but in the end she could see right through me.

"You're not happy for us, are you, Kim?"

"I am," I say weakly. "I'm glad that you guys are working this out. And I'm glad that you're having the baby."

"But what? You seem like something's bugging you."

"I don't know…" I pick up my water glass and try to think of something harmless I can say. "I guess it's a lot to take in. I mean, here my best friend is getting married, having a baby, and we haven't even graduated from high school yet. It sort of blows my mind, Nat."

She nods. "Yeah, it's kinda weird. I'll admit that. And it's not like anything I ever would've planned on. But you know what they say—when life hands you lemons…"

"Make lemonade."

"I just want you to be happy for me, Kim. For us. I really need you right now."

"I know." I force what I hope is a believable smile. "And I am here for you. You know that. And I'll do whatever I can to help. Have you guys picked a date for the wedding yet?"

"Well, as you can imagine, my mom would've liked us to have gotten married like yesterday. She's so worried about what people—mainly her church friends—are going to think. But I think everyone will know what's up, so it's not like we really have to rush it too much. And besides, celebrities, like Britney Spears, do this all the time. The thing is, I don't want to have to wear a maternity wedding gown, so I'm thinking maybe in September. What do you think?"

I think I want to scream. And the bit about Britney—

give me a break! Instead I bite my tongue and say, "September sounds good."

"Yeah, it's not so hot. And I was thinking maybe you could wear yellow or gold."

"I don't look very good in yellow," I say. Like it matters.

"Well, maybe orange then. I want a fall color."

"Will you get married in your church?"

"We haven't really decided. Ben said maybe his Uncle Tony would want to do the ceremony. And I guess that would mean your church."

"And Ben's parents are okay with it?"

Natalie frowns slightly. "They're still kind of struggling with the whole thing. It's not like we've really gotten their blessing yet."

"Oh."

"But that won't stop us." She brightens. "Ben says he's committed to this. He's ready to be a husband and a father. He knows it's the right thing to do."

"Uh-huh." I pretend to be very interested in the last remnants of my taco salad.

"I know this isn't going to be easy," Natalie continues. "But we've got to make the best of it."

I look up and smile. "You're right, Nat. And we will."

But as I walk back to the newspaper office, I just don't see how. For the life of me, I can't imagine two seventeen-year-old kids pulling off not just a marriage, but parenting an infant. It's just absurd. But I know enough to keep these thoughts to myself. Instead I pray for them. I pray that God will lead them and show them what's really right to do. And admittedly, I don't even know what that is. For all I know, they could be right on track. It just doesn't seem like it.

Twenty-one

Sunday, September 1

I'm actually glad that summer is nearly over. I think I need the routine of school in my life. Naturally, I wouldn't admit this to any of my peers, because they'd think that was totally weird—like how can she really like school? But I do.

The only drawback to the fact that it's now September is the BIG wedding, which actually won't be very big since only family and very close friends are invited—although the invitations haven't been sent yet. I'm supposed to help Nat with this little project tomorrow.

The wedding date is set for Saturday, September 21. Pastor Tony will officiate, and the ceremony will be in our church with a reception to follow in the basement. "A very inexpensive reception," Natalie's mom informed

Melody Carlson

us last week. "Everything about this wedding will be inexpensive."

"Caitlin is helping me with the details," Nat told me a couple of weeks ago. "She's like a wedding expert."

"Yeah," I said. "Her wedding was so beautiful." What I don't say is that Caitlin's wedding, in my opinion, was truly beautiful because she and Josh did it the <u>right</u> way. Unlike the backwards way that Nat and Ben are doing it. So many things that a maid of honor must not say.

But this is what I'm learning—as I watch my best friend doing things that I don't quite understand or accept—<u>it's her life, not mine</u>. And if she asks for my advice, I can give it—in love. Although I have absolutely no control as to whether she would take it or not. But I don't need to obsess over Nat's life, or what I feel certain must be a huge mistake. Because it's her mistake. Not mine. And for all I know, it might not be a mistake at all. It's not like I can read God's mind.

I guess I'm learning to <u>let go and let God</u>. I talked to Caitlin about this very thing last week when she invited me to have lunch in their new apartment—which I have to say is totally cool. And when I commented on her fabulous-looking decor, she just laughed.

"Compliments of Target and Beanie's thrift store finds," she confessed. "And a few goodies we picked up south of the border."

"Well, it looks awesome."

"Thank you." She picked up a bright-colored pillow and fluffed it. "We had so much fun unpacking all our wedding gifts and things after we got home from Mexico. It was just like Christmas!"

"I'm so glad you guys decided to come back."

"It was the right thing to do," she said as she set a homemade quiche in the center of a very chic-looking dining table. "A God-thing, you know?"

I nodded as I sat down. "Yeah, I think I do know."

Then she sat down and said a blessing. "Dig in."

After a few bites and some general catch-up kind of conversation, I decided to get to what was bothering me. "Can I be totally honest with you about something?"

"Of course." She buttered a piece of French bread. "And you can even have client confidentiality." She looked up and smiled. "If you need it, that is."

"I do. Thanks." Then I took in a breath. "It's about Natalie and Ben."

She nodded. "That was my guess."

"Well, I'm sure you've heard the whole story by now."

She nodded again. "Yes. Ben told Josh and me everything while we were still down at the mission. And I know it wasn't easy for him either."

"Ben's really trying to do the right thing. I don't know if he told you how messed up Natalie was after all this happened. She totally fell away from God and wanted an abortion...and there were times when I think she was even suicidal. It was awful."

"I'm not sure that Ben knew all that."

"She pretty much kept it to herself, well, and me."

"That's a lot to carry."

"I know. It was really getting to me." Then I give her a quick rundown of my trip to Florida and my last night there.

"That is so cool, Kim. What a great story!"

"Yeah, it was amazing. And it's helped me a lot in dealing with Nat. But still…"

"You're worried about her."

"I'm worried about both of them. I mean, I totally realize it's their lives and their problems, not mine, but I just think they're making a big mistake."

"You mean by getting married?"

I nodded without speaking.

"Okay, can I have confidentiality too, Kim?"

"Of course."

"We're not convinced it's the right thing for them either. Josh has really been counseling with Ben since we came home. Actually with both of them. But Natalie, well, she's in a tough spot being pregnant and all. We understand how that could make her feel really desperate."

"Totally desperate. She was a basket case."

"Right. And like you said, it's their decision, not ours. We're just trying to give them the information and tools to help make sure they're making the right decision."

I wanted to make sure we were really on the same page here. "So just because they're going to have a child, you guys don't think that means they have to get married?"

"We don't think that two wrongs can make a right. Not that we know it's wrong for them to get married. But we do see some red flags."

"Yeah. So do I." I sighed.

"So, if it makes you feel any better, we're not back behind the curtains pushing for them to get married."

"It does make me feel better."

"I think all we can do is to speak the truth in love—when they're ready to listen—and to pray for them. After that, we just have to support them and love them and hope for the best. I mean, it's entirely possible that God can redeem this whole thing, and that they'll be happy together."

"Miracles do happen."

Caitlin laughed. "Yes, they definitely do."

"And I'm afraid it will take one to make this work."

"And that's why we need to just let go sometimes, Kim. Let go and let God. I mean, after you've done everything you believe He's called you to do—and done it in love—well, then it's time to step aside and just pray."

So I'm trying to follow Caitlin's advice. Not just about Nat and Ben either. I'm trying to apply it to all areas of my life. I can see that I've been kind of a control freak in the past. And look where that got me—almost certifiable.

Because when you get right down to it, we can't control much of anything. Well, other than ourselves and our own personal choices. The rest is up for grabs. And if we're really trusting God, really believing that He has

our best interests at heart—then what's to worry about?
Let go and let God.

Okay, it'll probably take me a lifetime to really get
that. But at least I'm off to a good start.

Reader's Guide

1. Besides the death of her mother, Kim had a lot of stress in her life. Do you think this helped or hindered her grief process? Explain why or why not.

2. How did you feel when you noticed Matthew and Kim drifting apart? Did you want them to continue dating? Why or why not?

3. Do you think it's right for Christians to date nonbelievers? What kind of challenges would result from that kind of relationship?

4. What did you think of Matthew's relationship with his grandfather? Was it a good step for Matthew to agree to attend the school his grandfather recommended? Explain.

5. Were you surprised to learn that Natalie was pregnant? If you were her close friend, what would you have said to comfort her?

6. After losing her mother, Kim's role with her father changes. Why do you think that is?

7. Despite her previous views, Natalie decides abortion is the only option for her. Why do you think she changed her position on this? How would you have advised her?

8. Kim was extremely stressed by circumstances in her life. How do you handle extreme stress? Kim went to her grandmother's house to unwind. Where do you go to renew your spirit?

9. Why do you think Ben and Nat decided to get married? What do you think they should do?

10. Kim learned that she could control very little in her life—and yet this experience led to an extremely cool encounter with God. Why do you think that is? Have you ever experienced anything like that?

experience
Melody Carlson
real life. **right now.**

Diary of a Teenage Girl Series

Kim

Enter Kim's World

JUST ASK, Kim book one

"Blackmailed" to regain driving privileges, Kim Peterson agrees to anonymously write a teen advice column for her dad's newspaper. No big deal, she thinks, until she sees her friends' heartaches in bold black and white. Suddenly Kim knows she does NOT have all the answers and is forced to turn to the One who does.
ISBN 1-59052-321-0

MEANT TO BE, Kim book two

Hundreds of people pray for the healing of Kim's mother. As her mother improves, Kim's relationship with Matthew develops. Natalie thinks it's wrong for a Christian to date a non-Christian. But Nat's dating life isn't exactly smooth sailing, either. Both girls are praying a lot—and waiting to find out what's meant to be.
ISBN 1-59052-322-9

FALLING UP, Kim book three (Available February 2006)

It's summer, and Kim is overwhelmed by difficult relatives, an unpredictable boyfriend, and a best friend who just discovered she's pregnant. Kim's stress level increases until a breakdown forces her to take a vacation. How will she get through these troubling times without going crazy?
ISBN 1-59052-324-5

THAT WAS THEN.... Kim book four (Available June 2006)

Kim starts her senior year with big faith and big challenges ahead. Her best friend is pregnant and believes it's God's will that she marry the father. But Kim isn't so sure. Then she receives a letter from her birth mom who wants to meet her, which rocks Kim's world. Can her spiritual maturity make a difference in the lives of those around her?
ISBN 1-59052-425-X

Log on to www.DOATG.com

Diary of a Teenage Girl Series

Caitlin

Check Out More Great Fiction
by Melody Carlson

DIARY OF A TEENAGE GIRL, Caitlin book one
Follow sixteen-year-old Caitlin O'Conner as she makes her way through life—surviving a challenging home life, school pressures, an identity crisis, and the uncertainties of "true love." You'll cry with Caitlin as she experiences heartache, and cheer for her as she encounters a new reality in her life: God. See how rejection by one group can—incredibly—sometimes lead you to discover who you really are.
ISBN 1-57673-735-7

IT'S MY LIFE, Caitlin book two
Caitlin faces new trials as she strives to maintain the recent commitments she's made to God. Torn between new spiritual directions and loyalty to Beanie, her pregnant best friend, Caitlin searches out her personal values on friendship, dating, life goals, and family.
ISBN 1-59052-053-X

WHO I AM, Caitlin book three
As a high school senior, Caitlin's relationship with Josh takes on a serious tone via e-mail—threatening her commitment to "kiss dating good-bye." When Beanie begins dating an African-American, Caitlin's concern over dating seems to be misread as racism. One thing is obvious: God is at work through this dynamic girl in very real but puzzling ways, and a soul-stretching time of racial reconciliation at school and within her church helps her discover God's will as never before.
ISBN 1-57673-890-6

ON MY OWN, Caitlin book four
An avalanche of emotion hits Caitlin as she lands at college and begins to realize she's not in high school anymore. Buried in coursework and far from her best friend, Beanie, Caitlin must cope with her new roommate's bad attitude, manic music, and sleazy social life. Should she have chosen a Bible college like Josh? Maybe...but how to survive the year ahead is the big question right now!
ISBN 1-59052-017-3

I DO, Caitlin book five
Caitlin, now 21 and in her senior year of college, accepts Josh Miller's proposal for marriage. But Caitlin soon discovers there's a lot more to getting married than just saying "I do." Between her mother, mother-in-law to be, and Caitlin's old buddies, Caitlin's life never seems to run smoothly. As a result, the journey to her wedding is full of twists and turns where God touches many lives, including her own.
ISBN 1-59052-320-2

Log on to www.DOATG.com

Diary of a Teenage Girl Series

Chloe

Diaries Are a Girl's Best Friend

MY NAME IS CHLOE, Chloe book one

Chloe Miller, Josh's younger sister, is a free spirit with dramatic clothes and hair. She struggles with her identity, classmates, parents, boys, and whether or not God is for real. But this unconventional high school freshman definitely doesn't hold back when she meets Him in a big, personal way. Chloe expresses God's love and grace through the girl band, Redemption, that she forms, and continues to show the world she's not willing to conform to anyone else's image of who or what she should be. Except God's, that is.
ISBN 1-59052-018-1

SOLD OUT, Chloe book two

Chloe and her fellow band members must sort out their lives as they become a hit in the local community. And after a talent scout from Nashville discovers the trio, all too soon their explosive musical ministry begins to encounter conflicts with family, so-called friends, and school. Exhilarated yet frustrated, Chloe puts her dream in God's hand and prays for Him to work out the details.
ISBN 1-59052-141-2

ROAD TRIP, Chloe book three

After signing with a major record company, Redemption's dreams are coming true. Chloe, Allie, and Laura begin their concert tour with the good-looking guys in the band Iron Cross. But as soon as the glitz and glamour wear off, the girls find life on the road a little overwhelming. Even rock-solid Laura appears to be feeling the stress—and Chloe isn't quite sure how to confront her about the growing signs of drug addiction...
ISBN 1-59052-142-0

FACE THE MUSIC, Chloe book four

Redemption has made it to the bestseller chart, but what Chloe and the girls need most is some downtime to sift through the usual high school stress with grades, friends, guys, and the prom. Chloe struggles to recover from a serious crush on the band leader of Iron Cross. Then just as an unexpected romance catches Redemption by surprise, Caitlin O'Conner—whose relationship with Josh is taking on a new dimension—joins the tour as a chaperone. Chloe's wild ride only speeds up, and this one-of-a-kind musician faces the fact that life may never be normal again.
ISBN 1-59052-241-9

Log on to www.DOATG.com

Here's a Sneak Peek at Kim's Final Diary—*That Was Then...*

Monday, September 2

School starts tomorrow. My senior year. And I'm glad. I look forward to my classes and to seeing teachers again. I'm sure an even bigger reason I want school to start has to do with Natalie. I'm so sick of hearing about how happy she and Ben and the baby are going to be...how beautiful their wedding's going to be...how God has truly blessed them in an unexpected way. And I can't let on to her how I still think it's a great, big, fat mistake for two seventeen-year-olds to get married. Or how it's really hard playing the role of her best friend these days. No, I just have to smile and act like everything's peachy. Yeah, right.

The only thing that keeps me from totally losing it is my relationship with God. Seriously, I feel like I'm starting to depend on Him for everything these days. There's a Bible verse (2 Corinthians 12:9) that says God gets glorified by our weaknesses because we have to lean on Him, and as a result, He gets to really shine in us. I think that's been my personal theme verse this past summer.

And I really have to kick this verse into gear on days like today. Here I was thinking how I was just going to hang around and enjoy the last day before school. Maybe get a few things done at home, practice my violin, answer some letters in my column—but then Nat calls up and insists we go shopping. And she doesn't mean back-to-school shopping. No, that would be too obvious. Nat wants me to go with her to look for her wedding dress and my maid of honor dress. What an honor!

And never mind that all the last-minute back-to-school shoppers are out in hordes, or that the parking lots are packed full, or that it's nearly a hundred degrees out. We still <u>have</u> to go shopping.

"We can't keep putting this off," she tells me when she calls late this morning.

"Just for week?"

"Fine," she says in an aggravated tone. "But just so you know, I already invited Caitlin to join us today. If you don't want to come, well, I'll just tell her you're too busy and she and I will do it on our own."

I let out a long sigh. "I'll come."

"Great! It'll be fun, Kim. Just the three of us."

So it's agreed. And although I try to be a good sport and I keep my smiley face on throughout most of the day, I am so ready for this to be over. After wearing out the traditional mall where all the wedding gowns are out of Nat's price range, we head on over to an outlet mall. And this final stop seems to show the most promise. At least when it comes to price tags. Caitlin learned about this little discount shop when she was looking for her own wedding gown. Of course, as it turned out, her good friend Beanie Jacobs, who goes to this big New York design school, created a gown that was a perfect dream. Caitlin looked like a princess in it.

"What about this?" Nat says as she finally emerges from the dressing room with the saleswoman just behind her. It's about the hundredth dress she's tried on today. And I have to say that her stamina (especially in light of being pregnant) is rather impressive.

Caitlin and I both stand back and study the cream-colored satiny dress as Natalie moves in front of the big three-way mirror.

"The sweetheart neckline looks very nice on her," the saleswoman points out.

"Not bad." The good news is that I actually mean it this

time. "It's simple but elegant, and that style really seems to suit you, Nat."

She pats the small rounded belly that's become a bit more obvious lately. "And the way the waistline is cut high like this sort of disguises the baby. Don't you think?"

"Is there room to get bigger?" Caitlin asks. "Steph warned me that the baby will really start to grow after the fifth month. She said to make sure you get a dress with a little room, just in case."

Nat checks the dress around her waistline. "I think it'll be okay. I mean, it's only three more weeks to the wedding. You wouldn't think I could get too big in that amount of time."

Caitlin shakes her head as she looks at the dress more closely. "I don't know, Nat. Just to be safe, you might want the next size up. Why don't you just try it and see."

"Shall I get you the next size up?" the saleswoman asks with a hopeful expression, like she thinks we might be getting out of her hair soon.

Natalie seems to consider this as she looks at herself in the mirror again. I can tell she's not totally sold on this particular wedding gown, that it's not really her dream dress. But this isn't exactly a dream wedding either. And it's quite possible that the marriage will turn into a real nightmare. But, selfishly, I want to end the shopping now. I do not want to go looking for wedding dresses again.

"It looks so great on you," I tell Nat. "It's the best one you've tried on all day. Imagine it with your hair up…you'll look so elegant, so grown up."

Her eyes light up at this. "Grown up?"

I nod eagerly. "Yes, don't you think so, Caitlin?"

"It does make you look older…"

Nat holds her blond hair up with one hand and gives the dress one longer look. "Okay, I'll go ahead and try the next size up."

The saleswoman smiles. "I'll get it for you."

As it turns out, the larger size isn't all that much bigger than the other one, but enough that we all think it'll be the best choice.

"And the price is really reasonable," I point out. "Even less than what your mom budgeted."

Natalie turns around again, checking out her dress from every possible angle.

"Since Ben is tall," Caitlin says, "you two will look very regal together."

Nat looks at me. "Cesar's not that tall. With your height, Kim, you guys will be just right together."

"Is that who Ben finally decided on for best man?" I ask.

"Yeah. Since Josh finally agreed to perform the ceremony. Ben and Cesar have really been getting close lately."

"This will be Josh's first wedding." Caitlin smiles. "Pastor Tony really had to twist his arm to get him to do it."

I suppress the urge to point out that it makes perfect sense for the youth pastor to perform the wedding ceremony for two seventeen-year-old youths. How appropriate.

Finally, it's decided that Nat will get the creamy satin after all. As we're leaving the store and Natalie is gushing to Caitlin about how perfect everything is going to be and how great it will be to have Caitlin as her sister-in-law, I notice what I think is a shadow of doubt cross Caitlin's countenance. And I'm guessing that, despite her sweet nature and positive attitude, she's still struggling with this marriage. Probably just as much as I am. After all, Ben is her little brother. And although he has as much to do with Nat's pregnancy as she does, Caitlin must be feeling somewhat protective of him.

And as I sit in the backseat, I can't understand why one of the "adults" in either Ben's or Natalie's lives hasn't put the brakes on this whole crazy thing. I mean, what are these people thinking? Even my dad is appalled by the craziness of this. And it's not like it's his daughter getting married either. I seriously doubt that he'd ever allow me to do something like this. Even if I were pregnant.

"Have you guys found a place to live yet?" I ask absently. Okay, maybe I do want to stir the pot just a little. Make Nat think a little further than just the big wedding day. And I absolutely refuse to discuss the honeymoon with her, although she's already informed me that they'll probably stay at a cabin in the mountains that's owned by friends of Ben's family. She thinks it'll be so romantic.

But I'm imagining this rustic animal-infested shack with a smelly outhouse and no running water. Okay, I'm a terrible excuse for a friend. But it's only because I love Nat, because I care about her future. And possibly because I'm a realist.

"Oh, yeah, I meant to tell you. Josh's mom knows an older couple who need house sitters until next spring," Caitlin says as she turns down the street where Nat and I live.

"Really?" Nat sounds hopeful.

"I think Josh gave Ben the number, and he's going to talk to them."

"That sounds good." Then Nat gets quiet. "But that would mean we couldn't really get settled...couldn't have our own things."

Okay, I'm wondering, <u>what things?</u> But at least I don't say this. I mean, I know that Nat and Ben have registered at a couple of stores. But from what I've heard from Nat's mom, the wedding's going to be pretty small. Which reminds me, I wonder if being maid of honor means I'm supposed to plan a wedding shower or something to that effect. I lean back into the seat and let out a little groan. When will the madness end?

"You okay?" asks Nat.

"Just a little carsick," I say, which isn't entirely untrue. I'm in a car and I feel sick.

"Almost there," says Caitlin.

Caitlin drops us off, and we both thank her. I make a mental note to call her later for some wedding shower advice.

Sheesh, I'm only seventeen. I shouldn't have to be doing all this. Of course, as I walk into the house, I realize that Nat shouldn't either. But then it seems as if she's enjoying it.

In the family room, I tell Dad all about our afternoon of shopping "fun" and set my purse down on our new leather couch. Dad and I replaced a few things—in an effort to move on in our grieving process over mom. "Everything about this wedding feels all wrong to me too, Dad."

"It seems a hard way to start a life together…getting married because of a baby. I just don't know…"

And suddenly I remember my grandma, Dad's mom, and the surprising story she told me down in Florida last summer. I look at Dad and wonder if it's the right time to tell him about this. But he's replaced his reading glasses and is already opening his book again. Maybe some other time.

After I head up to my room, I do a double check on the things that I've already laid out for school, because I'm tired of thinking about how my best friend is ruining her life. Everything seems to be in good order. And so I decide to check my e-mail and maybe answer a letter for my column.

Dear Jamie,

My mom has been married six times so far. My dad was number two in the lineup, and they got divorced when I was a baby. Her marriages last two to three years, although they seem to be getting shorter. And every time she gets engaged, she says, "This one is going to be the one." Anyway, she's about to get married again. She calls this dude her "lucky number seven," but I can tell he's a loser like the rest. I'm seventeen, and this will be my senior year, but I'm sick of this game. I'd like to move out, but I'm not sure I can handle it. I have a part-time job, but I don't know if it's enough to support myself with. What should I do?

Tired of Stepdads

Dear Tired,

I can understand your frustration. But I also understand your hesitancy to move out. Here are my questions for you: 1) Is there another relative who you might live with during your last year of high school? 2) Or do you have a good friend with understanding parents who might let you stay there? 3) If you really want to move out, do you have enough money for a rental deposit? 4) Have you estimated what it will cost each month, making a budget that includes things like rent, food, utilities, clothing, travel costs, etc.? 5) Have you asked a school or church counselor for advice? 6) Last but not least, have you told your mother how you feel and asked for her help in making this adjustment?

I know that being on your own could look tempting right now, but it could end up being like jumping from the frying pan into the fire. Maybe you should do what you can to get yourself ready to move out (like saving and planning a budget) while you give yourself time to see whether or not your mom's made another mistake.

Just Jamie